THE ICE CHIPS AND THE STOLEN CUP

THE ICE CHIPS
AND THE
STOLEN CUP

Roy MacGregor and Kerry MacGregor
Illustrations by Kim Smith

HarperCollins*PublishersLtd*

Published by HarperCollins Publishers Ltd

First edition

HarperCollins books may be purchased for educational, business,
or sales promotional use through our Special Markets Department.

HarperCollins Publishers Ltd
Bay Adelaide Centre, East Tower
22 Adelaide Street West, 41st Floor
Toronto, Ontario, Canada
M5H 4E3

www.harpercollins.ca

Library and Archives Canada Cataloguing in Publication

Title: The Ice Chips and the stolen cup / Roy MacGregor and Kerry MacGregor;
illustrated by Kim Smith.
Names: MacGregor, Roy, 1948- author. | MacGregor, Kerry, author. |
Smith, Kim, 1986- illustrator.
Identifiers: Canadiana (print) 20190222344 | Canadiana (ebook) 20190222352 |
ISBN 9781443459990 (hardcover) | ISBN 9781443460002 (ebook)
Classification: LCC PS8575.G84 I246 2020 | DDC jC813/.54—dc23

Printed and bound in the United States
LSC/H 9 8 7 6 5 4 3 2 1

For anyone *who wants to play this magical game.*
You are welcome here.
—Roy MacGregor and Kerry MacGregor

To the people who make the Stanley Cup shine
brightly, as if it were new, after all its adventures.
—Kim Smith

CHAPTER 1
Riverton

Edge cringed as feedback from the hockey announcer's microphone bounced off the boards and echoed across the Riverton Community Arena:

"Ice Chips goal by number 17, Ekamjeet Singh!"

The large crowd in the far corner of the rink—the Ice Chips' families and friends—cheered wildly. The rest of the people in the arena either clapped quietly or openly booed.

"Assisted by number 97, Lucas Finnigan, and number 33, Nica Bertrand!"

The applause grew louder when it was announced that Nica had an assist—a rare accomplishment for a goaltender. Nica—known as "Swift" to her teammates—had caught a long wrist shot, dropped the puck onto her own stick blade, and fired it hard to centre ice. That's where Lucas "Top Shelf" Finnigan had snared it, carried it over the blue line, and dropped it to his linemate Ekamjeet, also known as "Edge." Edge then used a nifty toe drag to fake out the defence and another one to draw out the goaltender, and finally backhanded the puck into the net as gently as if he were passing a butter tart across a table.

This was Edge's new "tuck play"—a move he'd used to score over and over again ever since he'd seen Chicken do it when they met at the Calgary Olympics. His slick goal, his third of the game, had put the Chips up 5–4 over the Orangeville Orcas with less than ten minutes to play in the semifinal.

"Nice one!" Lucas said excitedly, patting Edge's back as the Chips' top scorer made his way to the bench to drink some water.

"Yeah, nice *teamwork*," said Edge with a smile. He glanced up at his parents, sister, and grandmother, who'd come out to watch the game.

Just then, another "Boo! BOOOOOO!" erupted in the stands.

Every Ice Chip on the bench knew where those boos were coming from: the mouths of Jared and Beatrice Blitz and their buddies on the Riverton Stars. The Chips' main rivals, and the only other competitive

U9 novice team in Riverton, had come out to watch this semifinal match to see which team they'd play in the final: the Orcas or the Ice Chips.

And as usual, they'd brought their bad attitudes with them.

"Hey, show-off!" yelled a mean, nasally voice as Edge tossed his water bottle back beside the bench. "You try to score like that on us and you're going through the boards!"

Edge didn't have to turn to see who was doing the yelling. It was Jared, the more annoying of the Blitz twins. None of Edge's teammates would ever call him a show-off. Matías Rodriguez—the Chips' second goalie, known as "the Face"—was the one who was always bragging and making jokes to get attention. Edge was more the kind of player who made sure all his teammates got a chance with the puck. Coach Small had even called him captain material.

Throughout this match, the Blitz twins had been coming around the Ice Chips' box, chirping and trash-talking the players. Mr. Blitz, the Stars' wealthy coach and the twins' father, didn't even seem to care what his top players were doing. They'd been picking on Edge a little more than the others today, either because of his goals or because each time he'd tapped the puck into the net, his grandmother—who'd been a hockey superfan ever since she'd moved to Canada from India—had yelled and cheered louder than anyone else in the stands. Even the Blitz twins now knew that "*Mahriaa shot, keeta goal!*" in Punjabi meant "He shoots, he scores!"

And there was nothing that made them madder than hearing that an Ice Chip had shot a puck into their net—even if Edge's grandmother *had* called that black disk a "rubber tiki" in her cheers.

"There's still time for LOSERS LIKE YOU TO LOSE!" Jared shouted at Edge, and then snickered along with his teammates. There were a few Stars who weren't seated with the Blitz twins: Shayna and Nolan Atlookan, another brother and sister who were coached by Mr. Blitz, seemed to be keeping their distance. Nolan, who was deaf, couldn't hear the mean things that the Blitz twins were saying, but he *could* read lips. Each time Jared gave Edge a thumbs-down or placed his hand on his forehead in the shape of an *L*, Nolan gave the Ice Chips a shrug and a smile of encouragement.

As Edge got back into position on the ice, he kept his head tucked down onto his chest, his face slowly burning red. The Orcas thought it was because he was shy about scoring so much; the Stars thought it was because of the booing. But only Lucas knew the truth: Edge was checking the tie on his hockey pants, afraid that while he'd been concentrating on putting the puck in the net, the laces might have come undone.

Just like Lucas, Edge had a secret he didn't want anyone to know. And he wanted to make sure it stayed hidden.

* * *

For Lucas, it had all happened by accident—*the first time*.

A few weeks ago, Lucas was late for their second match in the league semifinal—a game against the Lake Placid Miracles. He'd been helping his parents clean up their store, and they'd simply lost track of time. The Chips' centre had to throw his stuff into the back seat of the van with lightning speed so his dad could race him to the Blitz Sports Complex for the game.

In the back of the vehicle, Lucas scrambled to dress, twisting his body like an acrobat as he struggled to put on his hockey underclothes. He knew he'd have to put on all his equipment during the short drive if he was going to make it in time for the puck drop—all but his skates.

Somehow, in the dark and confusion and in that tight awkward space, he'd managed to get his underwear on, followed by the rest of his equipment.

Lucas arrived in the dressing room just as Coach Small was starting his pre-game speech. The coach gave him a sharp look, but without a word, Lucas hurried over and began putting on his skates. He'd made it!

And then something happened during that game against the Lake Placid Miracles. The "miracle," it turned out, was Lucas himself. He scored four goals (two more than Edge) and led the Chips to a 6–2 victory!

Lucas had never scored four goals in a game. Not even in Swift's driveway when the Face—who was often more interested in talking about himself than blocking shots—had come out to play net.

In the dressing room after the match, as Lucas stripped off his socks, shin pads, and pants, several of the Chips had come up to fist-bump or pat him on the back. Maurice Boudreau—whose hair was still sweaty from his hard work out on the ice—came over to talk.

"You, uh, made a mistake," Maurice, the big defenceman known as "Slapper," said carefully. He was keeping his eyes on the ground.

"What do you mean? I just played the game of my life!" Lucas asked, confused. He shook his head as he tossed his hockey shorts onto his bag and reached for his regular pants. *Is Slapper still complaining that he never gets to shoot on net? Or is he jealous?*

"It *has* to be a mistake, right?" Slapper asked, smiling, as the tips of his ears turned red.

Alex Stepanov—the little Russian-speaking kid called "Dynamo"—was soon blushing, too. He was giggling and staring at Lucas's hockey pants.

"Unless . . . is that another superstition of yours?" Slapper asked with a little giggle of his own. "I mean, is what you had *under there* supposed to be lucky?"

"Under what? Under where?" Lucas asked looking at his pants, still confused.

"Exactly—*underwear*," said Lars Larsson, pointing at Lucas's butt. "*This* is your superstition? Wearing underwear that's all flipped around?"

Lucas's cheeks turned the colour of tomatoes when he looked down to see that his blue-and-white-striped underwear, the pair he'd had to put on in the car—in the dark—was *inside out and backwards*!

The most embarrassing mistake ever!

And yet, he'd played such a great game . . .

So the superstition had stuck. For every single practice. Every single match.

Wayne Gretzky put baby powder on the blade of his stick before taping it. Patrick Roy won four Stanley Cups while talking to his goalposts as if they were alive and helping him. And Phil Esposito wouldn't stay in any hotel room that contained the number thirteen.

Lucas, the Chips' (now official) team captain and the most superstitious kid in Riverton, had an underwear thing.

And because this was the semifinals and the Chips were nearing a chance at the trophy, Lucas had made sure his best friend Edge had an underwear thing, too—at least until the end of the playoffs.

Underneath Edge's expensive, well-cared-for equipment and Lucas's stinking hand-me-down gear, the two Chips had their underwear on *inside out . . . and backwards*!

✳　✳　✳

The seconds ticked down on the old scoreboard clock in the Riverton Community Arena. With just under two minutes left in today's semifinal game, the Orcas pulled their goaltender in favour of an extra attacker and began to press hard.

Swift was playing brilliantly in goal, moving side to side to stop shots as the Orcas began pounding pucks at her as hard as they could. She made glove saves, stick saves, saves when she was down on her butt and couldn't even see the shooter. It was a spectacular performance by the Ice Chips' goaltender.

At one point, Swift blocked a hard shot and Edge gobbled up the rebound. He raced up with Lucas trailing, and everyone expected Edge to drop the puck to his teammate, who had also been having a pretty good game. (Thanks to his underwear, of course.) But Edge tricked them all by sending a lovely saucer pass over the stick of the last Orcas' defenceman.

The puck slid to Slapper, who was now in all alone with a chance to put the game out of sight. The Orcas' goalie was sliding over on his pads to cover the short side, but Slapper still had room both over and under the goalie's blocker glove. He raised his stick to take the shot.

All he had to do was fire the puck into the net.

But he didn't do it!

That's because Lucas, afraid that Slapper was taking too long, swooped in and grabbed the black disk before the defender's stick could make contact. Lucas tried to shoot the puck back to Edge, but the Orcas' defenceman, who had fallen, slid over the puck and smothered it, completely by accident.

Slapper banged his stick on the ice in frustration.

"We could have used that," Edge said to Lucas. "Why did you take it? Slapper might have put it away!"

The whistle blew just as the buzzer sounded to end the semifinal game. The Ice Chips had held on, thanks to Edge, Lucas, and Slapper—and more clutch goaltending by Swift. After the on-ice handshake between the teams, the Orcas repeated the team cheer they'd hollered at the start of the game. Only this time, their hearts weren't in it:

Do we play hard?

YES!

Do we play hard?

YES!

Who are we?

ORCAS!

Who are we?

ORCAAAAAS!

The Ice Chips had just beaten them 5–4.

Unsurprisingly, Edge was named first star of the game. He was roundly cheered by one corner of the rink, but loudly booed by a section on the other side of the ice.

Many of Coach Blitz's players, again led by Jared and Beatrice, had also booed.

This win had just put the Chips into the final against the Stars!

CHAPTER 2

WHOOOOOOSH! Wuuuuh-OOOOOSH!

"Do you actually think the hockey gods *like* that one?" Edge asked as another giant whoosh sounded from the small washroom stall in the Chips' dressing room. Most of the Chips had already left to collect their newly printed hockey cards from the arena's skate-sharpening stall, but Lucas had stayed behind.

As usual, Edge had been sent back to get him.

Lucas was flushing his hockey stick in the toilet over and over again for luck, just as the Ottawa Senators' centre Bruce Gardiner had once done in the hopes of ending a scoring slump. It had worked for Gardiner, so why not for Lucas?

"You know that we *won*, right?" asked Edge, leaning in the open dressing room door. "I mean, the game's over. The equipment's off. You can stop flush-ing, or whatever you're doing."

It wasn't so much the flushing that was getting to Edge, but the fact that his best friend *already* had about a million superstitions. *Why did he need more?* Every home game, the Chips' centre would rub his lucky quarter, run his hand along the ledge of the skate-sharpening shop, straighten a picture frame that hung beside it, and squish his face up against his team's glass trophy case so he could drool over what was inside. The case held a photo of an old Ice Chips team lifting the championship trophy in the air, but *no actual trophy*. The Chips had won the Golden Grail only that one time—in 1989, back when the Riverton coaches were just kids themselves.

Over the years, the Grail had gone to the River-ton Stars a few times, but for the past three seasons, it had lived many miles away, in the display case of the Orangeville Orcas.

Edge, Lucas, and their teammates had never even had a shot at it.

Until now.

The Riverton Ice Chips had just beaten the Orcas.

If they played their absolute best against the Stars on Saturday, that championship trophy could be theirs!

Is that *what's making Lucas's superstitious brain go so wild?* Edge wondered. While he'd been playing his heart out, living the Canadian hockey dream for his entire family, Lucas (whose family had played the game for generations) had been thinking about the Blitz twins, flushing toilets, and flipping his underwear inside out. Sometimes Edge didn't see how two players who played the game so differently could both hope to make the NHL, but they *did* hope. Sometimes they hoped so hard it hurt—that's partly what made them such good friends.

"Look, *Top Shelf*, why don't you practise your shot, stretch your legs, or retape your stick? Do something that might actually help. Or make up a cheer for our team. Coach Small says we should have one for the final," Edge suggested. The noises behind him in the hall were growing louder—the other Chips were celebrating their win and their new hockey cards—but Lucas didn't seem to notice at all. Tianna Foster, known as "Bond," and Swift were now just outside the door, comparing the cards they'd already traded with their teammates.

"It's not the final that's freaking me out," Lucas complained quietly as he leaned out the stall door with his hand on the flusher. "Not yet, anyway. It's the practice! Didn't you hear what Coach Small wants us to do?!"

"Ha! I can't believe my sister looks so fierce on her card!" Swift said loudly as she burst out laughing in the hall. "You'd think Sadie's been playing hockey for years!"

"She's unstoppable!" Bond giggled. "Dynamo looks awesome, too. Totally pro. Check it out."

"Wait, *Top Shelf-onator*," Edge said, not worrying if the girls in the hall overheard him. "You mean you're *afraid* of playing *half ice*?" For weeks, the Chips' coach had been talking about holding some practices where they'd pretend the rink had been cut in two, making two smaller rinks. The idea was that more players would get a chance to handle the puck, which meant they'd get more shots on net. Basically, more practice.

"Of course I'm afraid of half ice!" Lucas grumbled as more voices joined the girls in the hallway. "I mean, how is playing *half ice* going to help us prepare for our *full-ice* final against the Stars?"

"If you want an entire rink to yourself, that's *easy*,"

said Bond, turning the corner with a mischievous smile.

"Just take SCRAAAATCH for a spin," Swift added, a little too loudly. The Chips' goalie was feeling reckless—her team had just won!

Lucas knew that Scratch, the small ice-resurfacing machine they'd found hidden in their arena, could make a perfect clean sheet of ice. But he also knew that Scratch's floods could open a portal that would send him and his friends flying through space and time.

"Right! If you want a different rink, you can always leap through time to—" Edge started, but he quickly closed his mouth.

"Duuuuuuudes!" Slapper shouted as he, too, entered the dressing room with one of his own freshly printed cards stuck to his forehead. "We got hockey cards! Just like the pros! *Wooo-hoo!*"

Blades followed behind him, then Lars. Everyone was back to get their equipment.

"Yeah, Edge, you're right—it's *time to* . . . get my hockey cards!" Lucas said awkwardly, trying to cover. His acting was becoming almost as awful as Edge's.

Lars gave him an odd look and then turned to the big Chips' defenceman. "I'm not sure the pros have

ever made *that* face for the camera," he said, flicking Slapper's forehead card before leaning down to grab his bag.

Slapper had made the goofiest grin he could in his photo and was holding his stick like he was playing a guitar solo—but that was Slapper. He was a lovable bear of a kid who was always ready to make the others laugh.

"Or *that* face," Lars said, pointing at Lucas's actual face as he swung his bag up onto his shoulder. "Lucas, you look like you're about to explode! Either you've got a secret to tell or you'd better go back into that bathroom stall."

"They've got a private club," Slapper jumped in, looking a little sad. Lately, he'd grown suspicious of the way Lucas and his friends had been sneaking around and whispering, but this was the first time he'd said anything. "What's the big secret, anyway?"

Swift's and Bond's cheeks flushed red.

Inside Edge's head, all he could think was, *Don't say time travel! Don't say time travel!*

Lucas gulped, thought about Scratch and then about his inside-out underwear—his *other* big secret—and immediately went back to flushing.

❋ ❋ ❋

"He should just get over it, don't you think?" Bond asked her friends loudly the next afternoon, causing the school librarian to hush her for the third time.

Edge didn't want to get in trouble, so he just nodded back. Swift gave an uncomfortable shrug.

"*Half ice* is not *full ice*," the Chips' goalie explained quietly.

She and Edge were keeping their eyes on the librarian while Lucas set up his usual mini-sticks game between the stacks. Bond, who was a little annoyed that *everything* was always about Lucas, was colouring on the side of her shoe.

Lucas had been obsessing over the Chips' training since their win against the Orcas. And now none of his friends knew how to tell him the *other* news about tomorrow's practice: that their team would be sharing the ice with the Stars. Coach Blitz's high-end rink was getting a laser show installed to make it even fancier for the final on the weekend. So while the technical work was being done, the Stars and the Chips would share a rink like they used to.

"No duh, half ice isn't full ice," Bond answered

back with a smile. "But it's still ice." She dropped her marker and jumped to her feet. "I got this—I know what Lucas needs to hear."

The Chips' centre was lying down on his stomach between the stacks with a hockey card in one hand and a button he'd borrowed off the librarian's desk in the other. Bond watched him pull back his card and take a weak bendy shot with the button before she spoke.

"Hey, Lucas, what if we actually *did* leap again? You wanna?" Bond said close to his ear. She was trying to get the words out quickly so none of the other students would hear her. "I missed seeing my dad helping at the Olympics. And Edge missed that leap, too. Let's all make the jump. Let's get out of here—let's go!"

"I'm waiting for the mini-sticks," Lucas said, trying to see past her to where the kids' backpacks had all been piled. Bond rolled her eyes. "When do you want to do this?" he asked, lining up another shot.

"Tonight," said Edge, moving in beside Bond.

"My dad told me that all the grown-ups will be at the technical meeting tonight at the Blitz Complex," said Swift, joining in. "That includes Quiet Dave!"

Lately, none of the Chips had wanted to leap. Quiet Dave, the guy who looked after their rink, had been too hard to get rid of, and they'd been too busy with semifinals. They'd also been distracted with other projects: Edge had started playing basketball with his dad, Lucas had started doing little jobs at his parents' store, and Swift had started her track-and-field training again. Swift's doctor had made some adjustments to her prosthetic running leg, and now she was one of the fastest runners in the region.

"Well, it depends," said Lucas. "*Who's* leaping?"

Just a little farther down the stacks, Sebastián "Crunch" Strong and Dylan "Mouth Guard" Chung were riffling through books in the do-it-yourself section. Lucas guessed it was probably for the Fix-it Club his parents had started at their Whatsit Shop. Mouth Guard was touching everything and getting on Crunch's nerves—even though the Chips' math nut had his face so close to his tablet he looked like he might blow his nose in it.

"You, Bond, and Edge are," said Swift, twisting her mouth to the side and holding her arm out. Carefully, she slipped something from her hand into Edge's. "Here—I made a copy of the rink keys a few weeks ago. I've got track practice tonight, so they're all yours."

"C'mon, Lucas! Leap with us. Have a little fun," Bond said, clapping her hands. She was speaking quickly, like she was ripping off a Band-Aid with her words. "Then you can forget that the Blitz twins will be at our practice tomorrow."

"THEY'LL WHAT?!" Lucas started, but he was cut off.

"Wait—*leap*? Into what, a pool?? I never get what you guys are talking about anymore!"

It was Slapper, who'd just returned with the four Montreal Canadiens mini-sticks Lucas had asked him to get from his bag. And with him was Lars.

"Edge? Lucas?" asked Slapper, looking a little hurt.

"Yeah, what are you guys whispering about this time?" asked Lars.

CHAPTER 3

Edge's back tire skidded on the gravel as he and Lucas abruptly stopped their bikes in front of the Riverton Community Arena. They'd been pedalling as hard as they could—even with their equipment bags on their backs. Edge's bike was high-end and could handle it, but the chain attached to Lucas's rusty bike frame had given out.

"My chain's off," he said, shaking his head. Up until now, their plan had gone well: they'd hidden their hockey sticks in the bushes after school, told their parents they were hanging out at Swift's house (her sister, Blades, said she'd cover for them), and passed Quiet Dave on the road while he was making his way to the other rink.

Now they just needed Bond.

And maybe some tools to fix Lucas's getaway ride.

"Hey, I'm here!" Bond shouted as she rounded the corner into the parking lot on her skateboard. She was pushing hard with her back leg, trying to keep up her speed. "I'm here, but all I've got are my skates," she said, tapping her backpack. "My parents were getting too suspicious. I had to leave my equipment behind."

"That'll do," said Edge with a smile. "Hide your bike in the bushes, Lucas. We'll fix it after we leap back."

Edge didn't want to admit it, but he'd been dreaming about this trip ever since he'd missed the last one. Travelling through time was Lucas's *escape*, his place to hide when life got tough—almost like a secret clubhouse. But for Edge, it was an *adventure*—it was living history! Each leap helped him learn more about the roots of hockey and the players who'd helped build the game. This was history he could hear, smell, feel—and it was better than any movie, better than any game on a screen.

"I'm still going to put on all my equipment. You?" Lucas was asking Edge as Bond pushed opened the dressing room door and nearly fell flat on her face!

"What the—?" said Bond, in shock. "I just tripped over a ... *book*?!"

Mouth Guard was in their dressing room, sitting on the floor. He was playing with Crunch's little model of the rink and had a dozen library books spread out in front of him: *The Art of Time Travel, How to Take Apart a*

Small Engine, and *The 10 Best Ways to Flood Your Rink*.

"It's not me, I swear. It's . . . Crunch," Mouth Guard sputtered, stumbling over his words. "He picked the lock at the Zamboni entrance."

"Oh no," said Edge, putting everything together.

"Please don't tell him I—" pleaded Mouth Guard, his neck turning red and splotchy. But it was too late. Lucas had already taken off running.

❉ ❉ ❉

"What in the world are you DOING?!" Lucas was the first to yell—the first to freak out.

By the time Edge reached the boards near the Zamboni chute, Lucas was already frozen in his tracks. His eyes were the size of hockey pucks, and his fists were clenched tight.

"How *could* you?" Edge whispered, staring at the sight in front of them.

Crunch was there at the mouth of the chute, on his knees. He had a screwdriver in one hand and a library book in the other. And there were pieces of Scratch scattered all over the ground.

Crunch, the Ice Chips' amateur engineer, had taken apart their time machine!

"How could you be such a . . . such a . . . a *STINK-O-SAURUS*?!" Edge barked, unable to contain his anger. Normally he hated name-calling, but he couldn't stop himself.

"Stink-o-saurus, eh? How do you spell that?" Crunch asked, barely looking up. He was working fast, although none of the other Chips knew what he was doing.

"You spell it with an enormous stink cloud!" Lucas answered, crossing his arms.

"Oh my, you've *broken* him!" said Bond, clasping her hand over her mouth.

"Do you even know how to put all that back?" Edge asked nervously. It was as though Scratch's robotic guts had all spilled out.

"*Sí, sí,*" said Crunch. "According to the calculations I made using my model, our rusty old Scratch will soon be cleaning the ice ten times faster! Didn't you notice he was having trouble with his turns the last time you leaped?"

"What? *No!* Who cares?" said Lucas. He looked like he was going to cry.

"What if by fixing him, you're breaking the magic?"

asked Bond, saying aloud what everyone else was thinking. "What if we can't time-travel anymore?"

"Wait—he's *gone*? You *killed* him?!" asked Lucas, his eyes pleading.

"Of course not!" exclaimed Crunch, but he didn't sound too sure of himself.

"There's only one way to find out if Scratch still works," said Edge, turning to his two leap buddies. "We're going to have to try him out."

❊   ❊   ❊

Once the flooding machine was reassembled, Lucas pushed the orange button on the remote control, and the Chips waited.

Pthu-pthu-pthu-pu-huzzzzzz!

At first, Scratch wouldn't move. And then the machine, which was only the size of a ride-on lawn-mower, began sputtering and wobbling around the rink. Moving . . . but *backwards*?

Phhhhriiiit-phroooo . . . Zeee-beeep! Zjjjjjjjjooooop.

Scratch quickly spun in a circle, and then kept spinning and spinning—like a dog chasing his tail or a broken amusement park ride. Steam was coming out of his engine, and he looked like he was about to spin off into the rafters.

"THIS ISN'T GOOD!" shouted Edge, shaking his head.

Bond couldn't take her eyes off the little malfunctioning robot, but Lucas couldn't look at all.

The three would-be leapers were all standing at the open door in the boards, skates on and ready to go. That is, if time travel were still possible. Thanks to Crunch and Mouth Guard's ridiculous fix-it scheme, this could be the end of their adventures!

If Scratch can't flood the ice properly, Edge was thinking, *we won't be going anywhere tonight.*

Or maybe ever.

But Lucas had an idea.

"Crunch! Mouth Guard!" he yelled, his eyes now open wide.

The Chips' fix-it guy was sitting in the stands, typing on his tablet. And Mouth Guard was walking up and down the rows of seats, counting his steps and humming to himself.

"What if it's the remote control that's broken and not the flooding machine?" asked Lucas, remembering a conversation he'd overheard while helping in his parents' store. "What if you've been fixing the wrong part?"

"Impossible!" said Crunch, shifting his glasses to the top of his head. "But . . . possible. Let me see if I can use my tablet to run him."

Crunch pushed a few buttons and then pushed a few more, and Scratch stopped spinning. The resurfacing machine moved forwards, then backwards, stuttering a little. And then, very slowly, he started to clear the ice, as carefully as a gymnast dipping her toes on a balance beam. One half circle at a time.

"Are *you* controlling him?" Bond shrieked, excited.

"No!" said Crunch. "All I did was push the reset button."

Soon, Lucas and Edge were staring at that same irresistible, mirror-like surface they'd fallen in love with on their first leap. It was glistening in the overhead lights. It was magical.

And again, it was calling them.

"He's working!" Lucas declared. "I'm getting on the ice!"

Mesmerized, he stepped slowly onto that hard, clean sheet—just as Scratch stuttered.

That's when *someone else* suddenly slid into view across the rink's centre line.

CHAPTER 4

Lucas, Edge, and Bond gasped as a girl dressed in a heavily layered old-fashioned dress smashed right into Lucas's shoulder, knocking him off his skates. He couldn't figure out where she'd come from. It was almost as though she'd fallen out of the sky!

The girl had puffy sleeves and a smear of something black across her right hip—was it soot?—and her light brown hair was tied back in a soft bun. She was half-running, half-sliding across the ice. She looked terrified.

"Whaaaa . . . whoa! *Whoa!*" she shouted as her carefully laced leather boots sent her sliding toward the blue line. It was as if she were running on banana peels. She had one arm out in front of her, ready to brace herself against the boards, and her other arm gripped a large silver bowl tightly to her chest.

"Is this really happening?" Bond asked, her eyes wide in shock.

Blinking in the brightness of the arena, the girl spun sharply to see who'd spoken . . . and fell flat on her butt.

Her legs were splayed out before her and her soot-streaked skirt was half inside out, but she looked ready for a fight, ready to defend herself. The Chips could see that under all those layers was an exceptional athlete.

"These strange lanterns!" the girl cried in a British accent. She was looking around as though she'd never seen rink lights before. "Where have I—"

"Don't be afraid," said Lucas, skating slowly toward her. "We're not going to hurt y—"

"Grab her!" Crunch yelled from the stands. "We've got questions to ask!"

The girl looked at Lucas, and he could see terror in her light blue eyes. *Is she running from something? Or someone? Is it us?*

"Oh no! Now *you* want to steal this? I already told you, it belongs to *my family*!" the girl shouted, scrambling to her feet and clutching her bowl tighter. She was breathing heavily; she was panicked. "You can't just . . . where on God's green earth have I—"

"Careful. Easy now," said Edge, who had stepped on the ice. He, too, was skating toward her.

"No! No! I won't let *anyone*—" cried the girl as she slid away from them, backing up toward the centre line.

"What's she holding?" asked Bond.

As the girl's skirt tails crossed the red line, they seemed to fade into the reflection of the rink lights. *Or become invisible?* It was as though they were being *pulled* into the wormhole.

A second later, the girl was feeling it, too. She looked frightened. She was fighting against the force, but she didn't seem to be winning.

Is she being pulled back to where she came from? Edge wondered. He was worried for her.

"Whaaaaa—AHHHH!" she screamed, looking at the three Ice Chips. As her arms reached toward the kids for help, she let go of her precious bowl and it went flying across the ice. Her eyes grew wider as she realized what she'd done—and that's when the kids heard a loud slurping sound. There was a flash of light as the girl was sucked completely over the rink's red line.

She'd vanished!

All that was left was the silver bowl, spinning on the ice in front of the Chips.

Spinning and spinning toward the boards!

"Catch it! Stop it!" yelled Bond, but Edge was already diving across the ice, sliding toward the shiny silver bowl with his gloves stretched out in front of him.

* * *

When Lucas arrived home, he was more nervous than he'd ever been in his life. He was barely able to turn the door handle, he was shaking so badly. He'd kicked off his shoes, rushed past the dining room (where his father was cleaning up), and raced up to his bedroom as quickly as he could. He was desperate to stay out of his parents' sight.

"*You're* back late. How was doing homework at Swift's?" Lucas's mom called over from Connor's room, where she was reading Lucas's little brother a story.

"Great!" Lucas yelled back from the glowing dome that his bed sheets had become. His room was dark, but under his sheets he had a flashlight. "We learned a ton of history. Tell you tomorrow. I already brushed my teeth! Goodnight!"

Of course, Lucas had no intention of telling his parents what had really happened: that he'd snuck into the arena, seen the dismantling of a flooding machine, been knocked flat on his butt by a girl from the past, and somehow walked home with her prized possession.

One large silver bowl.

Lucas was tracing the grooves around the silver object with his flashlight when Swift called.

"Top Shelf, I asked you to *read* it! What does it say?" Swift yelled through her comm-band, the watch-like walkie-talkie worn by every kid on the Ice Chips team. She'd buzzed Lucas once she arrived home from her track-and-field practice, and now she was buzzing again. Lucas had already told her about Crunch taking Scratch apart, and about the girl who'd appeared and then been inhaled back into the past like dust into a vacuum cleaner. (*Did that wormhole really take her home?*)

"Dominion . . . Hockey . . . Challenge Cup," Lucas read carefully. "It looks like some kind of award or a prize. Or I guess it could be even be a flowerpot."

"Do you think it's valuable?" Swift asked, feeling sad that she'd missed all the action. "If it's not, you could probably just recycle it with that chain Crunch

pulled off your bike. Or drop it off at the Salvation Army. We can't give it *back*, can we?"

"Crunch forced me to take a new chain from his 'fix-it' supplies—otherwise, I'd have kept the old one," said Lucas, offended.

He and Edge were mad at Crunch, but they'd still needed his help to get home. Outside the arena, Crunch and his screwdriver had done wonders on Lucas's bike (yet another item inherited from Lucas's cousin Speedy). That's where they'd come up with their plan to hide the silver bowl from Quiet Dave, their parents, and the rest of the Chips until they could figure out how to send it back into the past.

Lucas was chosen to be the shiny award's very first babysitter.

"This thing isn't old, you know," he said as he turned the bowl around in his hands. "Well, it's old, like, *history* old, but it looks brand new. It's shiny and perfect, and there are barely even any finger smudges on it."

"Any clue who the girl was? Or how to find her? That *is* your plan, right?" asked Swift, sounding a little jealous.

"No, not yet," said Lucas sadly. "But we *have* to find her. We should be able—"

BUZZZ-SHEEEP-ZZZZZZZ!

It was Edge on the other channel. Lucas pushed the face of his comm-band and patched him into his conversation with Swift.

"Crunch says he's figured it out—how to fix Scratch!" said Edge, sounding like he'd just run all the way from Crunch's house. "We've got our practice tomorrow, but on Thursday we'll sneak back into the rink. *That's* when we'll leap."

"Bond has singing lessons with her sisters on Thursdays," said Lucas. "She can't come."

"Well, *I'm* in," said Swift. "Quiet Dave will be at the Blitz rink with my dad, setting up for the final on Saturday. We'll have all the time we need."

"You think the fix will work?" asked Lucas.

"It *has to*," said Edge.

"Fine, then. Let's do it!" said Lucas with determination in his voice. Without even thinking, he breathed fog on the cup and polished it with the edge of his sheet.

"Oh, Lucas?" Edge said excitedly. "Don't forget to bring the bowl with you."

* * *

"Wow, that is the HUGEST bowl in the whole entire UNIVERSE!" Connor's voice was echoing through the house just as the Finnigans' doorbell rang. It was still early in the morning, but Lucas knew exactly who it was: Edge and Swift.

The three of them had decided that the only way to protect the silver bowl was to keep their eyes on it. Today, that meant taking it to school and then to their half-ice practice.

"Connor, *shhhh*," Lucas said, scolding his brother. "Why is your face always so loud? Don't say *anything* to Mom and Dad, okay?"

"Don't say about the GIANTEST bowl on the *planet*?" Connor asked, still at full volume.

Lucas whispered something in his brother's ear just as their dad came up from the basement carrying a laundry basket. He was answering the front door.

The Chips' centre had snuck down from his bedroom that morning to stuff the bowl into his backpack, but it hadn't fit. Now he was looking under the kitchen sink to see if there was a shopping bag that could carry it—that is, hide it. Connor, of course, had gone bananas the moment he'd seen the shiny object from his high chair.

"LU-CAAS? What's 'quiet as a ninja'?" Connor asked loudly, not understanding what his older brother had said in his ear.

Lucas just rolled his eyes and kept searching. He had to move fast. He was about to get caught.

"Cheeeeeerio-eeeeoooo-eeeOH!"

Connor, the kid who would *never* make a good ninja sidekick, had started singing. It was his way of asking his brother to shoot Cheerios into his mouth like mini hockey pucks. And luckily, this gave Lucas an idea.

"I didn't realize Lucas had something you needed for school," Mr. Finnigan told Swift and Edge as Lucas's friends followed him toward the kitchen.

"It's, uh, for a play," Swift said nervously. "It's a prop."

"She means a costume," said Edge using his talking-to-parents voice. "It's for a . . . knight. You know, one of those horse guys with the *jabby-jaberoo* things. It's a helmet."

Edge was acting out a jousting match (terribly) as he, Swift, and Mr. Finnigan walked into the kitchen to see Lucas, his chin dripping with milk, raising a spoonful of Cheerios to his mouth.

"Is *that* your helmet?" Mr. Finnigan asked, looking at his son's shiny new cereal bowl.

"It . . . *is*," said Edge, not knowing what else to say.

Swift wrinkled her nose in disgust, and Mr. Finnigan narrowed his eyes.

"Didn't your mom say no more Cheerios for a week, Lucas?" his dad said, shaking his head but smiling. During the Finnigan brothers' last game of cereal hockey, Lucas's elbow had knocked over a vase that had smashed and spilled all over some important papers—inventory for the Whatsit Shop.

He'd been grounded . . . from eating cereal.

"Wooo! Cheerios!" yelled Connor, whose chest was covered in jam. "Daddy, Lucas winned the big hockey bowl!"

"Ah, and it's an *award*, too!" said Mr. Finnigan, laughing as he walked back toward the basement stairs. "That bowl looks like it could be a lot of things. Maybe you could give Connor a bath in it when you're done with your play!"

"Ha! Poopy baby bum!" Connor said, cheering for the bath idea.

"But really, guys, that's thoughtful of you to gather up props for your play," said Mr. Finnigan, lifting his laundry basket. "I'm sure Mr. Small appreciates the help. You know, you three are turning into some nice human beings."

"Wait—we're *human*?" asked Edge, flattening his hands on his stomach as if he were Pinocchio becoming a real boy. "Human! Finally!"

"Wow, your acting is . . ." Lucas said with a chuckle, not daring to finish his sentence.

"A distraction," Swift said as Mr. Finnigan went down the stairs. "Put the bowl in here." She quickly handed Lucas her bright purple track equipment bag.

"You know, it does kind of look like a trophy," Edge said as he watched the zipper close.

"It's a fake—probably just a sentimental thing," said Lucas, grabbing the rest of his stuff to go. He then yelled up the stairs: "Mom, I'm leaving! Come watch Connor!"

"Well, the *real* trophy we want is the one that we'll win on Saturday, right?" Edge said, feeling pumped.

"Yeah, but we'll have to get through that horrible half-ice practice first," said Lucas as they filed out the door.

They could still hear Connor yelling as they walked down the driveway: "Poopy, *pooooopy* baby bum!"

CHAPTER 5

The teenage girl seated in the lobby of the Riverton Community Arena, selling tickets for Saturday's league final, gasped.

She'd never seen anything quite like it.

There wasn't even a game—the arena was being used for a simple half-ice practice—but the turnstile by the rink doors was spinning like a top. Parents of both the Ice Chips and the Stars were arriving all at once to cheer on their players.

At a *practice*!

Edge's family members, of course, were there, too. They were *always* there. They'd come out in India to watch Edge's father play professional field hockey, and now they came out in Riverton to watch Edge play ice hockey.

Edge's mother was speaking in English with his sister, Noor, but his grandmother was speaking Punjabi with his dad, who already had his fancy camera out. The grandmother—Edge's beloved *dadi*—was wearing her usual loose, pastel-coloured *salwar* pants and had a white scarf wrapped around her hair, but she also had on her lucky oversized hockey jersey. It had the Riverton Ice Chips' logo on the front and the number 17 under the name "Singh" on the back.

Edge might not be superstitious, but Dadi definitely was. She would do laundry only on Tuesdays (even Edge's stinky hockey underclothes had to wait!), and she made her grandson drink an extra-strong almond milkshake for breakfast on game days, just as his father had when he was in the field hockey pros. Edge's grandfather—Dada—wasn't always able to make it out to games since he'd broken his knee, but the Chips' forward didn't mind. There'd be plenty of videos for Dada to watch when the family got home to the house they all shared.

One by one, the players' family members filed through the turnstile, talking excitedly. Slapper's dad, who spoke French but often didn't say anything at all, was wearing his Montreal Canadiens hat. Lars's mom had come out, and Crunch's brainiac parents had turned up with their three other brainiac kids (each one with his or her nose in a book).

When Dadi moved past the ticket seller, she suddenly stopped, put her hand on the girl's shoulder, and said: "*Mahriaa shot, keeta goal.*"

The teenage girl stared at the grey-haired woman, utterly baffled.

Mr. Singh, who was walking behind his mother, leaned over to the ticket seller and smiled.

"She thinks the Chips are going to win," he said cheerily.

"It's not a game," the girl whispered, as if sharing a secret. "It's just a practice."

Mr. Singh smiled again. "Don't tell her lucky jersey that. My mother's convinced there will be a game tonight."

❖　❖　❖

Edge, Lucas, Swift, and Crunch were all nervous as they dressed, and it wasn't just because the Stars were in their arena. An hour earlier, right after school, Swift and Lucas had snuck into the rink in broad daylight with the goalie's purple track bag in tow.

Ever since the silver bowl had leapt ahead in time, the members of the Chips' "secret club" had been terrified that someone would see it and take it away from them—either because they'd think it was stolen or because they'd want to steal it for themselves.

"What do I do with it *now*?" Lucas had whispered after they'd made it through the rink doors. "We can bring the bowl into the dressing room while we dress, but then what?"

"We need to *see* the bag—or at least the spot where we hide it—to make sure it's safe," Swift said as her mind raced.

Suddenly, she clapped her hands as if an idea had exploded between them.

"That's *it*!" she said. "What is it that bank robbers and jewel thieves do in movies? They hide what they've stolen in plain sight, right?"

"What does *that* mean?" asked Lucas. "We're not in a movie!"

"You know, they wear the jewels or hide a stolen painting by hanging it on a wall," she said, struggling to keep her voice down.

"You want me to hide the bowl . . . in the *trophy* case?" asked Lucas, still confused.

"Oh, no way!" she said. "But I think you *should* bring it to practice. Put it somewhere where people can see it but won't notice it—and won't touch it. Put it where no player wants to go."

"The penalty box?" asked Lucas, scrunching up his nose.

* * *

The half-ice practice *was* indeed just a practice—at least, that's how it started out.

Quiet Dave had brought in a series of portable boards, long enough to separate the ice at the Riverton Community Arena into two parts: the Ice Chips on one half, the Stars on the other.

And Coach Small had worked out a half-dozen new drills for the Chips to use on their half of the rink. He had the Chips skate while stepping over sticks he'd laid out in front of them, almost like playing hop-scotch. It was a drill to work on foot balance. Then he had them stickhandle a puck through a traffic jam of other pucks. This was a difficult drill, but one that helped improve their control. Next, they had to work across the blue line, criss-crossing their skates as they "danced the line"—a drill to teach quick movements to the side and also balance.

Up in the stands, Edge's dad was filming every drill, and Dadi cheered whenever Edge moved up in the line to take his turn.

"MAHRIAA SHOT, KEETA GOAL!!!" she shouted whenever the drill involved shots on net.

Lucas's parents hadn't come out because they were busy working on some new Fix-it Club project at their store—finally putting some of his dad's mechanic skills to use. So Lucas instead watched Slapper's dad every time he looked up into the stands. Mr. Boudreau had seated himself in the corner and was keeping his head down, but Lucas could tell he was eager to see his son score some goals.

Slapper was waiting in line to do exactly that when, without warning, he turned and stared at Lucas with a look somewhere between anger and hurt on his face.

"How's your underwear?" the Chips' big defence-man asked. "Is *that* why you came to the rink early today?"

Lucas gulped. *How did he know? WHAT did he know?*

"Uh, no—I left for the rink early in case the chain fell off my bike again. To be sure I'd make it."

"The ticket seller said you *and* Swift were here before everyone else," Lars grunted from behind. "You guys are up to something. Why don't you let us in on it?"

"Or are we not good enough for your club?" Slapper asked, his face begging to be taken on by Lucas and his friends.

Luckily, it was now Slapper's turn for the stop-and-start shooting drill. Looking genuinely hurt, he took off after the puck. He did a few starts and stops, made a power turn, and then took his shot. The puck looked like it was going to ding off the crossbar, but somehow it turned in mid-air, like a curveball pitch in baseball, and was soon slamming clean into the back of the net.

Lucas looked up at Slapper's dad just in time to see a small smile cross his lips.

Edge, who was waiting in a different line, was watching the Stars practise on the other side of the portable boards. What Swift and Lucas had done with the strange British girl's bowl was making his hands sweat. If this was just a practice, the penalty box wouldn't be used. But if it turned into more than that, as Edge's grandmother kept insisting it would, then they'd really be in trouble.

Coach Blitz, who'd been skating around his section of ice, barking at his players, suddenly came to a stop near the Stars' bench and leaned an elbow on the boards. Soon, Jared was skating over to his father and whispering something.

A play? A complaint about half ice? Or . . . worse?

Lucas shot Edge a look.

Are we about to get caught? Edge wondered, just as Beatrice, on the other side of the line, thumped the boards in front of him and stuck out her tongue.

"We're going to have a game of shinny, bozo!" she shouted with a mean competitive smile.

CHAPTER 6

Coach Blitz had been furious about the half-ice practice. He liked to imagine himself as a big-time, big-league coach on *big* ice. And his kids, Beatrice and Jared—who seemed to think they were already halfway to the NHL—had been fuming, too. But they'd all known that with a final coming up, a practice on half ice was better than no practice at all.

So they'd said yes to Coach Small's idea.

And then, when the Blitzes had asked if they could turn that practice into a game, Coach Small had said yes, too. Why not? The teams could work on plays better playing four-on-four or three-on-three, rather than worrying about a crowd of ten full-ice skaters buzzing around the puck like bees in a rose garden. There would be more shots, more saves, more goals, more fun. To both coaches, it was a no-brainer—finally, something they could agree on.

On one side of the rink, a small game would be played; the other side would remain a practice and be handled by the teams' assistant coaches.

Coach Small quickly set some lines for the four-on-four scrimmage. He put Swift in net, of course, and named four skaters for the first shift: Lucas, Edge, Bond, and Slapper. They'd play against Jared, Beatrice, Shayna, and Shayna's brother, Nolan. The Stars were missing a goalie, however, so the Face was drafted to their shinny team for the evening.

"You look good as a Star," Slapper joked as the Face swapped his Chips' jersey for a Stars' one.

Playing around in his full-of-himself way, the Face was posing and grinning as if there were a photographer in front of him. *This* was the kind of behaviour that had earned him his nickname.

"You want my dad to take a photo?" Edge added, laughing.

"Only if your grandma promises not to yell *'Mahriaa shot, keeta goal!'* when the puck's down in my end!" the goalie answered with a smirk.

The Face, whose parents were also new Canadians—

but from Argentina, in South America—had always giggled when Edge's dadi shouted her cheer. Edge was never sure if the Face was laughing at her or was just uncomfortable with himself, but it had always got on his nerves.

Once all the chosen players were on the Chips' half of the ice, Lucas skated over to Swift with his eyebrows raised in alarm. Nothing needed to be said. Swift knew exactly what Lucas was thinking.

If this is now a game, what happens when a penalty's called?

The only good news was that Coach Blitz was the one with the whistle in his mouth. If someone went to the penalty box where the two Chips had hidden the silver bowl, it certainly wouldn't be Jared or Beatrice. The Stars' coach would never call a penalty on his darlings.

For the faceoff, Coach Blitz seemed to deliberately drop the puck so that his son had an advantage over Edge. Jared was able to turn so that he blocked the Chips' forward and then send the puck back to Shayna.

Shayna, who had once been a forward but was on the Stars' defensive line this season, took off on the half ice, stickhandling neatly. Edge moved to check her, and she used a tuck play—*his* tuck play—to slip by him as if he were a reflection in the glass, not a real player.

Shayna came in fast on Swift, dropped the puck from her stick blade to her right skate, and then kicked the puck back to her stick, causing the Chips' goalie to move with the puck. Swift was sliding hard along her crease when, without looking, Shayna dropped the puck back to where her brother was waiting.

Nolan had a completely empty net in which to tap the puck, making it 1–0 for the Stars.

Coach Blitz blew his whistle as if he were leading a parade, not refereeing a hockey game. Nolan made a sign to his sister, and they both started laughing.

"*P*, then *K*," Shayna said, explaining the letter signs as she glided past Lucas on the ice. "For penalty kill."

"But there's no penalty kill here," Lucas said, confused. "It's always four-on-four."

Coach Small had told them that for their half-ice game, any player who got a penalty would simply be replaced. No one would ever be down a player, which meant there would be no player advantage.

"Yeah, we know—no PK," said Shayna with a friendly smile. "But we kind of killed it on that open net anyway, don't you think?"

Lucas tapped Swift on the pads before lining up for the next faceoff. He could tell she was blaming herself—which was silly, because Shayna's little move would have fooled anyone.

He circled by Slapper before moving into the centre area for the puck drop.

"Slap, you set me up, okay?" Lucas said, grinning like the Face. "And I'll get it in the net."

Lucas didn't want to admit it, but what he disliked about half ice was that it gave the other players on his team more chances to shoot. Edge was already a far better scorer than he was, but Lucas was still a good skater. If his teammates improved their stickhandling and plays, who knew where he'd rank?!

Slapper nodded, saying he was ready to assist. He had a great shot—by far the best slapshot on the team—but he rarely tried to score in a game. He left the glory to the Chips' forwards.

Just before the puck dropped, Lucas looked over at Slapper and nodded meaningfully. Slapper quickly nodded back.

Lucas won the faceoff and got the puck back to Bond, who spun behind Swift's net. The ice surface was so much smaller that Beatrice Blitz was on her quickly, trying to check her, but Bond was able to clip the puck off the boards so that Edge now had it. He quickly flipped a backhand pass to Lucas.

Lucas came into the Stars' zone and curled back just as Jared Blitz was about to check him. Out of the corner of his eye, he could see Slapper on the far side of the half ice, his stick already raised to take the shot on net. Both Lucas and Slapper knew this was the Chips' best chance.

Jared had turned and was skating hard straight at Lucas, an angry scowl on his face. All Lucas had to do was get the puck where Slapper needed it.

Lucas *could have* passed the puck between Jared's skates and placed it perfectly for Slapper—so the defenceman could bring his stick down as hard as he could swing it, the puck taking off like a rocket into the top shelf of the net behind the Face.

But he didn't.

He could see Slapper's dad's eyes—ready, waiting. But he could also see that open top-shelf hole . . .

There was a shot, and *Lucas* wanted to be the one to take it. He could feel the tag on his underwear tickling his belly button, and he could already hear the shouts erupting in the stands: *"MAAAAAAHRIAA SHOT!"*

Feeling selfish but determined, Lucas lifted his stick—but Jared Blitz hadn't stopped coming! He hit Lucas with his shoulder, driving him back hard against the boards. Lucas's helmet hit the Plexiglas.

Craaaack!

The crowd went silent as he struggled to shake it off. This was novice; the games were no-contact. A few of the Chips' parents booed, and then *they* were booed by some of the Stars' parents. No one was happy.

Swift and Edge stared nervously at Coach Blitz to see if he'd actually make the call. Coach Small was watching, too. He raised his eyebrows, nodded, and then waited. Coach Blitz's face grew redder and redder, until finally, reluctantly, he placed his whistle back between his lips and blew.

A *penalty* for Jared Blitz!

❉ ❉ ❉

The Chips were up 2–1, thanks to Edge, when Slapper finally circled back around Lucas on the ice.

"*I* could have taken that shot," said Slapper, whose eyes looked puffy.

"I know," said Lucas guiltily. He'd stopped looking up at Slapper's dad—he didn't want to see the disappointment he'd caused. Instead, he had his eyes on Jared, who'd been acting funny ever since he got out of the penalty box.

"You don't let me do *anything*," Slapper continued, tapping his stick on the ice as he got into position behind Lucas. The space was so small that they could still talk easily. "I *can't* shoot on net. I *can't* join your stupid secret club. You probably wouldn't even let me wear my *underwear* inside out!"

"You can do whatever you want with your underwear," Lucas said with an awkward laugh, trying to sound relaxed. In reality, he was panicked. The worst person in the world had been sent to the penalty box— *their hiding spot!*

From the bench the Chips were sharing with the Stars for their half-ice game, Mouth Guard had heard the word "underwear" and was laughing so hard he snorted.

Out of the corner of his eye, Lucas could see that Jared was whispering something to Beatrice with a mischievous look on his face—Nolan saw it, too. *Can he read their lips?* Lucas wondered. Nolan made a sign in Lucas's direction, but Lucas didn't know what it meant.

Now it was Coach Small's turn to whistle. "Our time's up!" he suddenly called over to Coach Blitz, who was ready with the puck to start play again. "Dave wants to clean the ice!"

Coach Blitz nodded toward the arena's regular ice-surfacing machine, which was already coming out onto the practice side of the rink, and then skated away with the puck. He didn't look happy about the score. A Blitz—Coach Blitz, Jared Blitz, Beatrice Blitz, *any* Blitz—hated to lose.

"Everyone shake hands!" Coach Small called to the players as he exited the Chips' side of the shared bench with his bucket of practice pucks and his clipboard with the drills so carefully laid out. Coach Blitz had no clipboard with drills. He didn't like practices— just games.

Lucas wondered if Jared was going to chirp him again when they met in the handshake line, but when the Blitz twins got to him, they seemed almost joyful, delighted about something.

"Good game!" Jared said, with only a hint of sarcasm. He took Lucas's hand and shook it strongly.

"Good game, Lucas!" Beatrice said, smiling as if they were best friends.

Swift was pulling off her mask and heading toward the door in the boards when the Face started copying Edge's grandma's cheer again. There was a bit of a mean cut to his tone this time—but maybe he was just angry because he was on the team that lost? Bond glared at him and Edge just tried to ignore him. Hockey was how the Singh family had first connected to life in Canada; Edge was proud of Dadi, and no one could change that.

Lucas hadn't even noticed the Face because he was busy squinting toward Nolan, who was leaving through the Stars' gate. Nolan had given him a little wave, with his hand slightly behind his ear, but Lucas couldn't figure out what he was trying to tell him in sign language.

"So what's your secret club about? Just tell me," Slapper demanded, stopping hard in front of Lucas. "Does it have to do with the rink? With that model Crunch keeps carrying around?"

Lucas's cheeks flushed pink and his mouth dropped open. *Has Slapper actually figured it out? What will happen if the whole team knows about our time travel?*

"No, we . . . we are . . ." Lucas sputtered as he started skating backwards, pushing past Crunch and Mouth Guard, trying to get away.

None of the Ice Chips were watching as Jared turned away from the boards and skated back toward the penalty box.

* * *

Swift and Lucas were out of the dressing room before anyone else. They hurried back into the rink just as Quiet Dave and the ice-surfacing machine were making their final loop.

They ran along the walkway to the back of the penalty box, and Lucas leapt over the boards as fast as he could. He dropped down onto the bench, then onto the floor, and reached under the bench for the straps of Swift's purple bag.

"It's gone!" Lucas whispered to Swift, panicked.

"What do you mean, 'gone'?" Swift hissed loudly, her eyes wide.

"Gone gone!" Lucas said, his voice shrill and anxious.

"Look again! It's dark!" Swift was freaking out.

Lucas looked again, but there was nothing there.

He scrambled back up over the bench and the backboards and onto the walkway, where Swift was breathing hard, as if she'd just completed a dozen sprints of the ice in full goalie equipment.

"You kids lose something?" Dave asked, calling from the Zamboni chute.

With tears in their eyes, Lucas and Swift just shook their heads.

CHAPTER 7

"Let's go, let's go!" Edge cried as he and Swift rounded the side of the Riverton Community Arena the next evening, running full out. They were coming from the Zamboni entrance, where Crunch had been busy at work on Scratch.

"We're all set up! What are you doing? Get in there!" Swift said, huffing.

Edge had grabbed Lucas's bike and was rolling it into the bushes to hide it. "Crunch didn't want to tell you," he said, "but he went to your dad for help. With one part—an engine part. He told him it was for the Fix-it Club. That's what your dad was working on last night."

"And?" Lucas asked slowly. He was trying to look enthusiastic, but there was something weighing on his mind—the reason he was late.

"And your dad fixed it!" said Edge. "At least we know *one* part works fine."

Lucas shrugged and tried to smile. They were going to leap. That was the plan. The only problem was that they no longer had anything to leap *with*. The silver bowl was still in the hands of the Blitz twins.

Jared hadn't been at school today, and that was Lucas's first problem. So Lucas had had to talk to Jared's sister—horrible Beatrice. He'd begged her for the track-and-field bag, but she'd refused to tell him where to find it. She'd laughed in his face and called him a loser.

After school, Lucas had ridden his bike over to the Blitz Complex, thinking that Jared might be at the rink with his dad, even if he *was* sick. Many of the Stars had come out to help with the laser thing, and there were adults everywhere—Mayor Ward and a bunch of parents were helping with the more difficult parts of the set-up.

What if Jared shows them the bag? Or the bowl? Lucas had wondered as he checked the Stars' change room and poked his head in the door of Coach Blitz's office. *If the parents see it, Quiet Dave will know we've been leaping.*

Dave would probably take Scratch away. And then their leaping would be over for good.

Lucas decided he couldn't draw attention to the bag by demanding it—he couldn't chance it. He'd glared at Jared from afar and Jared had glared back, but that was it.

Unsure of how to tell his friends what a wimp he'd been, Lucas was already mounting his bike outside when he saw Nolan standing near the Zamboni entrance, behind Mayor Ward. He was giving Lucas that same odd wave he had at the end of their shared practice last night—his hand flat but his thumb tucked in front, waved slightly behind his ear.

"See you at the final," Lucas had mouthed back to him with a smile, not knowing what else to do. Nolan had shaken his head and done the wave again, but Lucas was already pedalling.

⁑ ⁑ ⁑

"Where *were* you after school?" Edge asked his best friend as the three Chips changed into their equipment in the dressing room.

"I . . . uh, okay! I didn't get it! I didn't get the bowl!" said Lucas, surprising himself with the truth. "I was afraid that Jared would try to show it off. A lot

of the jerky Stars were there—but Shayna and Nolan, too. Nolan gave me that odd wave again, and I didn't see Swift's track bag anywhere."

"What's odd about the wave?" Swift asked as she strapped a goalie pad onto her left leg—the one with the prosthetic attached just below the knee.

"It's not really that it's odd—I just don't know what it means," said Lucas truthfully.

"Well, I DO!"

Bond had just burst into the dressing room with her equipment bag over her shoulder . . . and Swift's track bag in her hands.

"This"—she made the same waving motion as Nolan—"is my name. *B* for Bond. And the movement behind the ear is for my braids. Nolan was saying my name."

"But . . . why?" Lucas asked, confused.

"Shayna and Nolan live on my street. I found this on my doorstep when I was leaving for my singing lesson just now. Nolan was telling you he had a plan."

Lucas and Edge couldn't believe it! Shayna and Nolan had taken the bag back from Jared, probably not long after he'd stolen it.

Was Jared too embarrassed to come to school? And was he glaring because he knew he'd lost his game?

"Do you think he looked in the bag?" asked Edge, worried what that could mean.

"Would *you* look in a bag you stole?" asked Swift.

He must have. Lucas was sure of it.

"Well, I'm missing my singing lesson now," said Bond. "So stop blabbing and let's do this."

* * *

"Okay, all aboard!" Crunch said with a nerdy little chuckle. He replaced the lid on Scratch's engine and stepped back with his tablet. The Chips' math nut pushed a few buttons on the screen, and soon Scratch was rolling onto the ice and drawing wet, glossy half circles on the white surface in front of him.

"He looks okay, don't you think?" asked Lucas, sounding like a pet owner talking to a veterinarian.

"Just a few last-minute checks . . ." said Crunch, as though he'd known what he was doing all along. "It all looks fine from over here."

"Can we go for it?" asked Bond. Crunch nodded proudly, so she, Swift, Lucas, and Edge stepped onto the ice one by one.

What an amazing secret we have here, thought

Edge. His blades cut into the hard surface as he followed the curve of the boards. He turned sharply and shot a spray of ice chips out in front of him. He felt guilty that they hadn't told the rest of the team about Scratch, and that Slapper felt so left out. But he also knew that this was a secret they had to keep.

The more people who knew about Scratch's abilities, the more dangerous this would become.

We can't ever let this wormhole fall into the wrong hands, he thought, watching the reflection of the lights dance on Scratch's flood.

"Are we ready?" asked Swift as she grabbed Edge's and Bond's hands. Lucas drifted over to the end of the line, holding on to Swift's track bag.

"Don't fiddle with anything while we're gone, okay?" Bond warned Crunch, sounding worried for the first time.

"I will if I have to!" Crunch shouted back with a defiant smile, taking his glasses off his head and sliding them onto his nose.

The four other Ice Chips took off skating. Edge, who was the fastest, pushed hard with his right leg, then his left, and pulled the others along toward the centre line.

"Close your eyes!" Lucas yelled, and the lights began to grow brighter ahead of them.

There was a flash . . .

And then they were *gone.*

* * *

"Don't let go of my *baaaaaag*!" Swift yelled in Lucas's direction. There was another flash, then another. *A glitch?*

The Ice Chips were turning, spinning.

They were being pulled away from the earth like kids on a Ferris wheel.

And then they were sinking down, down, down, as though the imaginary Ferris wheel had suddenly broken and come loose.

They were falling into the unknown!

CHAPTER 8
Unknown location

Lucas, Edge, Swift, and Bond landed with a thud in a pile of snow and were immediately surrounded by the sound of pounding hooves.

"WHOA! WHOA!" a man yelled, panicking. A woman with a large flowered hat screamed. They were sitting high up on a wooden bench, and the man was pulling back on two long leather cords. He yanked on them sharply, causing his horses—which were about to run the Ice Chips over—to swerve.

"That man's driving a sleigh! Like Santa!" Lucas yelled cheerfully after he and his teammates, who were covered in snow, had successfully rolled out of the way.

"*That's* what you were thinking?" asked Bond incredulously. She was still breathing deeply from their close call.

The Chips had rolled away from the road and onto a

flat strip of snowy land—where, to their surprise, they now saw two dozen wooden tennis racquets thumping their way toward them! The people watching the snow-shoe race were yelling, and soon the athletes were, too.

"Look out! Look out! LOOK OUT!!" a man in what appeared to be striped pyjamas called out. He was at the front of the pack of snowshoers, bounding with his right foot, then his left, as he leaped over the snowdrifts.

"Children, get away! Move!" the man behind him yelled as he elbowed his way into the lead.

"We're not safe here, either!" Edge called to Lucas, grabbing his friend by his jersey. "There are horses everywhere—and now we're going to be trampled by a snowshoe race!"

Part of what made Edge such a good hockey player was his ability to see what was going on around him. Even when he was skating with the puck, he was always aware of what the other players on the ice were doing. He knew if they were shifting position; he knew when they were coming after him.

"What *is* this—a fair?!" Bond asked excitedly as they squeezed their way onto the sidelines. "Oh, wow! There's a sled being pulled by dogs over there! And those clowns are throwing snowballs—I mean *actual* clowns!"

"Did you see the gigantic toboggan run?" asked Swift, who was pulling her boots from her backpack to change out of her skates. "And the candied apples and the hot chocolates?! *Everyone* here is having fun!"

"Yeah, you're right. But wow! *This* is the most *spectac-errific* thing of all, don't you think?" asked Edge. His eyebrows were raised so high that they'd almost disappeared inside his helmet.

In the distance stood the biggest, most elaborate castle the Chips had ever seen. It had turrets and rounded glass-like towers with flags sticking out the top . . . and it was made entirely of blocks of ice! Men in dark overcoats and women in skirts puffed out like upside-down tulips were moving in and out of the frozen palace, obviously impressed.

"It's almost glowing," said Swift as she watched the sunlight reflect through the bluish green masterpiece in Montreal's Dominion Square. "They must have used *thousands* of ice blocks to make that."

"*A Frosty Frolic*," Bond said with a giggle. She was reading a trampled-on pamphlet she'd picked out of the snow. "This, my friends, is Montreal's fifth annual Winter Carnival."

"Is that for real?" asked Lucas, looking at the

pamphlet, astonished. He pulled out his lucky quarter, which changed with each leap, to make sure he had it right. "We've landed in 1889!"

"Now *this* is worth the leap!" said Edge, looking at all the activity that was buzzing around them. His face was beaming.

* * *

"Get off the ice!" one person yelled, booing. Several more cried out, too, and soon the rest of the audience had joined them. The four Ice Chips had heard that there was a hockey game taking place in one of the buildings, and they'd happily moved with the flow of the crowd into an ornately decorated rink. But they hadn't noticed that the people they were following—all dressed in black pants, white shorts, and sweaters with *V*s on the front—were actually players!

"Why are we *always* in everyone's way here?" Lucas yelled to his friends over the booing. "These are players? How could we know? They don't even have any padding!"

"Must be what players wore back then—back *now*," said Swift.

"They've got sticks," said Bond, her voice sounding

worried. "They're definitely players. We'd better leave before they *make* us leave!"

As quickly as they could, the Ice Chips slid off the ice and pushed their way through the crowd until they found somewhere to stand.

"What is this? The first hockey game ever played?" Lucas asked jokingly. There were referees on the ice, but once the game had started, they didn't seem to do a very good job of stopping the players from fighting.

"No francophone players can fight like THAT, I tell ya! Look at those Irishmen go!" a man standing in front of them shouted. He was cheering on the players, who were yelling at each other in English, as two penalties were finally given. He'd obviously been enjoying the fighting. "But then again," he said, winking at Lucas, "there ain't many French Canadian players of *class*, you know."

The game was between the Montreal Victorias — the players with the *V*s on their sweaters — and the Montreal Hockey Club, whose sweaters were decorated with either flying wheels or bunnies. Neither Edge nor Swift could decide.

It was supposed to be a hockey game, but to the Ice Chips, it felt like what they imagined a night at the opera would be! There were large fancy sheets draped from the rafters, and flags hung from above; boughs of pine trees had been stretched over the ice like garlands! At rink level, people were standing to watch the game, even though there were no boards. And on a level above that, in what looked like balcony seats, the spectators were dressed like they were attending a royal dinner.

"Edge! Over there!" Swift said, nudging him with her elbow. She was nodding her head toward a couple who could, in fact, be royalty. They had special seats with the best view of the game. Even their children—several boys and one girl—were attracting attention.

At least, they seemed to be admired by the people around them on the upper level. The guy standing in front of the Ice Chips—the one who didn't like French players—kept calling them foreigners.

"The Queen's representative is *not* Canadian," the man explained in a rude tone when he caught Swift giving him her best side eye. "Not *everyone* can play this game. The Irish Canadians are wonders. The French are too slow. And the British . . . well, this game is too rough for them. *They* shouldn't even be here."

The man motioned toward the "royal" family as he

said this last sentence. And then, a second later, he was cheering on the Victorias again.

That is not true. Everyone can *play hockey,* Edge thought to himself angrily. *Anyone from any country, any background. And French players are some of the greatest. Even the British sometimes have—*

The British!

That's what Swift's nudge was telling him!

Up on the second level, the "royal" couple's daughter was transfixed, as though she'd never seen a game of hockey in her life. Edge could tell that she was falling in love, just as he had, while the game unfolded before her eyes. She was grinning. She was cheering.

This was the girl who'd appeared on the ice back in Riverton!

*   *   *

As the hockey game came to an end—the final score was 2–1 for the Victorias—the four Ice Chips decided to push their way through the crowd. This was why they'd leaped, after all: to give this girl and her family back their silver bowl!

The hockey players moved off the ice, and the rink

was flooded by people in costumes and masks—partiers who'd come out for the carnival's ice ball. The Chips were soon within just a few feet of the girl—so close they could almost toss her treasure to her.

"Excuse me! Hey, you!" Lucas called, realizing they didn't even know her name.

Swift tried to grab the girl's skirt, but she was sandwiched between two costumed partygoers and couldn't quite reach.

"Miss? Miss!" shouted Edge, trying to get her attention.

The girl turned and seemed to see the Chips, but she was simply pulling a feathered mask over her face as part of her costume. She took a few steps away from them and then disappeared into the crowd.

"You're not allowed to disturb the governor general's family," a man with a stern voice said, looking down at the Chips. Then he giggled. He looked like a guard, but a strange guard. More like a soldier in costume.

"Can we just—" Swift started, confused by the guard's smile.

"The governor general will be out watching the fireworks with everyone else," the guard said, motioning toward the door with a big grin. "If you go now, you can get a good seat. And you won't miss the surprise!"

* * *

It wasn't until the first spray of lights exploded above the ice castle that Lucas, Bond, Swift, and Edge realized their mistake. They'd squeezed through the outdoor crowd, still trying to make their way to the governor general's family, until Bond had decided they were too squished by all the people in winter costumes. They needed to catch their breath.

"We can't see anything from here!" she'd called out to her friends. "Follow me! There's an opening up ahead!"

That opening was the reason the Ice Chips now found themselves in the middle of what they could only describe as a snowy battlefield. To their right, red-jacketed soldiers were marching through the snow; blue soldiers were coming in on the left. The two groups of soldiers were marching toward each other—almost running—with angry looks on their faces, their bayonets out in front of them.

And the Ice Chips were smack dab in the middle of the fight.

"What is *with* this leap?" Lucas called as he crouched down in the snow, looking for a way to escape.

"This is way worse than being trampled by snow-shoers!" Edge said, looking up at the wall of audience members closing in behind them. He sounded scared. "They're going to kill us with those pointy *thinga-ma-whadayas*!"

It was an act. Of course it was an act—the battle was a play. But with the audience caught up in the dramatic scene before them, and with the display of booming fireworks above, no one would move to let the Ice Chips back through.

"We need to get out of here!" screamed Swift. "Are you sure this is all pretend?"

The soldiers were advancing on either side. They were concentrating so hard on their hatred for each other—or at least their make-believe hatred—that they didn't even see the four Ice Chips crouching in the no man's land that lay between them in the snow.

"If that crowd keeps pushing," said Bond, "even the actors pretending to be soldiers are going to get hurt!"

"Where do we go? Quick!" asked Lucas, panicked.

"The only place we can go is—" said Edge, oddly calm. This was how he'd always heard his grandfather had been when he was in the army in India. "Guys, we're going to have to storm the castle before they do!"

❊ ❊ ❊

The inside of the ice palace was even more impressive than the outside. There were chairs and tables, vases and sculptures—all made of ice. There was also an elaborate transparent staircase that curved up toward the second floor and then the third.

"What do we do now?" sputtered Lucas. *What if those soldiers are the ones who tried to steal the bowl in the first place? We still don't know who that girl was running from!*

"I think we've got only one choice here—we go up!" said Edge, trying to sound confident. "Then we hide. We don't want to get into trouble for being here."

The Ice Chips climbed the icy palace staircase as carefully as they could. Swift had wanted to put her skates back on, but the others thought they were safer in boots. They slowly made their way up, passing room after room of ice sculptures and icy furniture, breathing in the frozen air.

"This is the one!" said Bond finally. They'd reached one of the towers and a small room that had a rectangular ice bed covered in furs. In the corner, there was a gigantic (and obviously pretend) fireplace. "We'll hide

in there," she said, pointing confidently to the fireplace as though hiding in castles was one of her hobbies.

"Do you think they'll try to burn down the castle?" Lucas asked, clutching the bag with the bowl as a burst of white twinkling lights exploded with a crack and a fizzle outside the window.

"You mean *melt it*?" asked Edge, trying to keep his voice down. A burst of yellow fireworks lit up the room with a bang, then a whirling blue hue. "That's scientifically impossible—well, almost."

"This is just a play, remember?" said Swift as the crowd outside suddenly grew quieter.

"Hello, everyone! Can I please have your attention?" an actor's voice boomed. "We hope you enjoyed our fireworks tonight—and our battle. Now, before the costume ball continues, we're going to hear a few words from Canada's governor general. Ladies and gentlemen, Lord Stanley of Preston!"

This is Lord Stanley's silver bowl?!

Edge and Lucas looked at each other, their eyes wide ... just as the ice block at the back of the fireplace gave way!

CHAPTER 9

Swift, Edge, Lucas, and Bond had fallen through a trap door in the back of the icy fireplace, and they were now turning and rolling as they slid down some kind of icy chute, like a twisting slide at a waterpark.

"Nooooo!" cried Lucas as he reached out and tried to grab on to the slippery surface.

They were picking up speed.

And the light surrounding them was growing brighter . . .

"We're leaping again!" Bond called, but she wasn't sure the others could hear her.

Soon there was a flash and a sudden feeling of weightlessness.

Edge wondered how this could be happening. He wondered where the wormhole was taking them and when it would stop.

But Lucas's mind was on something else: *If that was Lord Stanley, and he's the owner of the silver bowl, then could this really be . . . ?*

* * *

The white light in front of the Chips' eyes seemed to be moving—almost stuttering, like Scratch had before the leap. *This has to be a glitch!*

The Chips felt the warmth before they saw the light. There was a flickering—a soft glow from a fireplace. And soon the room they'd landed in came into focus.

They were in a house, or maybe a cabin, standing in the shadows just beyond the semicircle of light cast by the fire. There was a woman seated in front of the fireplace, her shoulders covered in a multicoloured blanket made of yarn. In her hands, she held two long wooden sticks that she was moving and clicking together. She was knitting. And so was the young boy beside her. She was teaching him while they listened to a radio in French.

That accent—we're in Quebec, thought Lucas. *Is this the home of a hockey player?*

"There are goalie pads by the door," Swift whispered, elbowing Edge and Lucas, who were on either side of her. "They're made from potato sacks—look! They're the same as the ones we saw when we met Gordon in Saskatchewan."

"In *1936*," added Edge.

The boy, who was knitting a toque for himself, looked up at the sound of the Chips' whispers. He had a cut on his right cheekbone—maybe from a puck?— and another above his left eye.

The boy gasped, as if he was surprised, and then continued wheezing.

Does he have trouble breathing? Have we scared him into hyperventilating? Swift wondered.

Without looking up, the woman called out: "In your beds, children!"

She was keeping her eyes on her son—and on his heaving chest—but it seemed that this had happened many times before. The Chips' goalie wondered if the mother thought they were her other kids, sneaking out of their rooms to snuggle by the fire. She must have.

The boy, however, was looking straight at the four strangers from Riverton, his eyes wide.

Nervous, Swift opened her mouth to say *"Bonjour,"* but the Chips had already disappeared.

* * *

The hospital gurney came at the Chips so quickly that none of them even had time to move their toes.

"Sorry!" the nurse yelled as she pushed her empty hospital bed into a room down the long corridor.

Lucas checked his lucky quarter—it said 1961!

There's snow outside. It could be December, he thought, trying to put the clues together. *No, the Christmas decorations on these white walls are torn and falling off. It must be closer to the end of January.*

"We leaped into a *hospital*?!" Bond asked in shock, pushing her teammates up against the wall as a group of student doctors bustled their way past. "What are we doing *here*?"

Soon there were cries coming from the room the nurse had entered—a baby's cries.

A baby? Being born? Edge couldn't figure it out, either.

A man with a gruff voice—maybe the doctor?— cleared his throat and said, "Watch out, Brantford! This kid's going to be a hockey player!"

Then a woman's voice, slightly out of breath, laughed. "There you go, Walter. Someone to skate on your rink once we move into the new house!"

Lucas's eyes started to water. *1961? Brantford? A backyard rink? And a dad named Walter? This could only be—*

But the Chips were already travelling again.

❊ ❊ ❊

Sunlight stuttered like an old movie that had been loaded into the projector wrong.

Are we just changing channels on some giant TV? Is the wormhole breaking? Or coming apart? Edge didn't want to say it out loud, but that didn't stop him from wondering.

Bond could feel her stomach rising into her chest as the lights around them grew brighter again, faded, and then grew brighter still. The Chips were falling—*fast*.

They felt branches brushing against their arms and legs, and soon they were breaking through a gathering of trees—a forest—and crashing into the snow. They'd landed in the woods, on a snowy hill, and they were now *rolling* down it. They were out of control!

When they finally came to a stop—Lucas having lost his helmet and Edge a glove—the young hockey players found themselves lying in a soft snowdrift beside one of the biggest outdoor skating rinks they'd ever seen! On it, a game of shinny was underway.

"Oh, wow—now it's 1892!" said Lucas, who'd checked his quarter as quickly as he could. His hand was icy because of the cold, but he felt around in the snowbank anyway to make sure his backpack and Swift's purple bag had come with them.

"What does *that* mean—that it's 1892? That's before *everything*!" said Bond, standing and brushing the snow off her sweater.

"You're *right-a-roni*," said Edge. "There's no National Hockey League yet. Not even a Winter Olympics!"

"But those are *girls* playing hockey. Did you see? In dresses!" said Bond, looking around. "And there's some guy taking their picture. Is *that* why we're supposed to be here?"

"Aha, YES! I *know* this one!" said Swift, her cheeks turning rosy as she squinted at the scene in front of her. All the women on the ice, playing with no equipment and no protection, were wearing black old-fashioned

dresses—except for one. "Do you see that girl in the white dress?" she asked, pointing excitedly.

"Yeah," said Edge. "Is that—? Is *that* the girl from the Winter Carnival?!"

Bond's mouth dropped open as she realized who they were looking at once again: *The British girl with the bowl who crossed our centre line!*

"YES!" said Swift, her eyes growing wet with excitement. "I know who she is now. And what *this* is." She swept her arms wide to indicate the scene in front of them.

The hair on her friends' arms and necks suddenly felt charged with electricity.

"*That*, my dear hockey lovers, is Isobel Stanley," said Swift, grabbing Bond's hand and squeezing it tightly. "And this is the first photograph *ever taken* of a women's hockey game."

* * *

"Oh, goodness. You're early!" said the woman in the white dress, covering her windswept hair in embarrassment and pulling on a knitted hat.

The Ice Chips had walked over to the side of the

rink, where Isobel was sitting in the snow, taking off her skates. They could finally give back the bowl she'd left in Riverton!

"Early for *what*?" Bond asked, playing along as she watched the other skaters push their feet into their old-fashioned leather boots. They'd all played well, but none of them were dressed like hockey players. *I'd say we're more than a hundred years too early*, the Chips' defender was thinking, but she didn't dare say it out loud.

"Why, early for the tour!" Isobel said cheerily. "The woman who normally gives it has taken ill for the day and I promised to assist her. She said there would be some children in the group. I know I'm a little young, but I know plenty about Rideau Hall. I do live here!"

Lucas shot a look at Edge, then Swift, then Bond. *She thinks we're here for a tour?*

They couldn't give Isobel her precious silver bowl if she didn't remember them—or how they'd got her bowl in the first place. Maybe the wormhole had erased her memory? Or maybe . . . Had they landed *before* she took her trip to Riverton? None of the Ice Chips knew, but they knew enough not to ask.

They couldn't risk it.

The hand Lucas was using to hold Swift's purple track bag started to sweat.

What if she thinks we've stolen *her bowl?* He worried as his grip tightened. *What if she calls the police? Or the Mounties? Or Sherlock Holmes? Or whoever chases down bad guys back in this time?*

Lucas and his friends' dream was to *win* the Stanley Cup.

NOT to get arrested for stealing it!

CHAPTER 10
Rideau Hall—Ottawa, 1892

"Well, how do I *look*?" Swift said, laughing as she spun in front of an enormous mirror in Isobel's bedroom. While she twirled, the many-layered skirt she was wearing spread out into what was almost a full circle. Bond was there, too, dressed in the same elaborate outfit: a long, heavy cotton dress, thick stockings and a warm tightly fitted jacket. Bond's hair was in a bun on top of her head, but Swift still had her regular ponytail, even if it looked out of place.

"Who cares how you look!" Bond answered. She was almost doubled over giggling. She felt ridiculous, as if she was dressed in a costume, playing a princess. No one who played roller derby—Bond's old sport back in Chicago—would be caught dead dressed this way. In fact, no one would normally catch Swift or

Bond dressed like this, either, but it was the only way they were going to blend in out on the ice.

This was Ottawa in 1892.

And this was how a female hockey player dressed.

During the tour Isobel had given the Ice Chips of Rideau Hall, she'd shown them detailed tapestries and elaborate carpets, some beautiful handmade wooden furniture (all expensive antiques in the Chips' time), and many, many rooms with fancy light fixtures hanging from the ceilings. There were rooms for award presentations, rooms for formal dinners, and an ornate ballroom with a rounded ceiling that Isobel said had once hosted over a thousand guests. Lining the hallways were paintings, small sculptures, and trinkets from around the world, and right beside the ballroom, there was an indoor tennis court!

None of the Chips could deny it: Rideau Hall really *was* a sort of palace! Why wouldn't it be? The governor general's job was to represent the queen of England in Canada!

"These gardens must look spectacular in the spring," said Bond, pulling back the flowing drapes around the window in Isobel's bedroom so she could look at the snowy trees and bushes below.

"Oh, yes. They *do* look wonderful when the flowers are out!" said Isobel, but she was already slipping out of the room to see how Edge and Lucas were doing with the items she'd given them.

Isobel had told the Chips there was an indoor rink at Rideau Hall, and they'd asked if they were allowed to skate on it. The four hockey players from Riverton had *landed* in their equipment, but Isobel didn't know that. *How could she?* Swift had thought, smiling to herself. *And how could we have explained that our strange equipment is for hockey, but in the future?* When Isobel offered to get the Chips "properly dressed" to skate around, they'd felt they had no choice but to say yes.

"This place is amazing," said Swift once she and Bond were alone. "But when do we give the cup back? What do we do with it?" She was trying to see if her goalie pads could be attached underneath her dress, but she wasn't having much luck. *Maybe that's why Isobel gave me a pair of knee pads meant for cricket?*

"We do *nothing*. Not yet," answered Bond, keeping her voice low. "But I *do* have an idea . . ."

* * *

"You flipped them, right? You *promised*," Lucas said to Edge as he pulled on the padded pants Isobel had borrowed from one of her brothers. He was getting dressed as quickly as he could; he didn't want anyone else to see that he had his underwear on inside out and backwards.

But he *did* want to play well on that indoor rink.

And he needed his new good-luck charms to do that—both his and Edge's.

"Of course I did it," said Edge with an awkward smile. Lucas's underwear superstition was annoying him, but he didn't want to make his friend sad—even if all they'd be doing was skating around.

"Hey, do you think there are secret passages here, like in the ice castle?" Lucas asked, scanning the bookshelves behind him.

"Secret passages? Why? Are you looking to escape?" Isobel said, grinning as she entered the small library where she'd put the boys.

"Dressed properly" had turned out to mean thick gloves and knee pads, and sticks that were carved from wood, not at all like the composite ones Lucas dreamed about owning whenever his parents took him to the sports store. The sticks were shorter and there was no difference between right and left ones—meaning that none of them had a curve like the stick Edge depended on for his little tuck play.

Isobel seemed happy to be going out on the ice again. She'd told the Chips that she'd fallen in love with hockey the very first time she'd seen it, during a game at the Montreal Winter Carnival, at an elaborately decorated barn called Victoria Hall.

And the Chips, of course, had kept their mouths shut. They hadn't dared tell her they'd been there, too—enjoying the closeness of the game, the sizzle of the skates, and the sound of the puck moving from one player's stick to another's.

Remembering some of the hits the players took during that game, Lucas placed his hand on his head, to where his helmet would have been had he not lost it in the snow.

"I wouldn't worry about that now," Bond said loudly as she and Swift entered the library. She knew that Lucas was missing his helmet, but she didn't think any of them would be able to wear them. Not here. Not in *this* time.

"It wouldn't go with my outfit anyway," Swift joked before Edge and Lucas burst out laughing at the sight of the girls in their heavy dresses.

Bond gave them both a sharp look, telling them to smarten up and act like the dresses were normal—as they were for Isobel. But Swift just smiled, grabbed the boys' hockey sticks, and headed out into the hall.

❀ ❀ ❀

"Get away from there!"

Isobel was banging on a large window in the hallway, yelling at two boys who were standing near the doorstep below, shaking a parcel they'd found.

The Chips and their tour guide had stopped for a moment in the hall because Bond was asking about an empty glass display case—one she'd seen earlier on their tour. Isobel was telling them how she and her brothers had convinced their father to create a prize for hockey's best team—how he'd ordered a silver bowl from England and had the display case made, and how she and her brothers had been waiting impatiently for it to arrive at their home.

By Isobel's tone, the Chips were able to guess what was in the special package below: the Dominion Hockey Challenge Cup. Or as it was known to everyone in the future: the Stanley Cup!

It was one of the greatest symbols of the game they all loved . . . and these mean-looking boys were about to steal it!

"You—STOP! That belongs to my family!" Isobel yelled as she burst through the front doors of Rideau Hall, fuming. The two boys were walking away with her package, not even caring that she'd seen them.

"We don't want to go on that dumb tour our parents signed us up for. Why would we want a tour of a boring old government building—especially when it's just down the street from our house?" said the meaner looking of the two boys, motioning to where four grown-ups and a young kid were standing in the distance, looking at the view. "Just because our cousin wants to see it? No way!"

"But we'll keep whatever's in this box, thank you!" said the other one.

As the second boy started to unwrap and open the box, Lucas let out a loud gasp. If *he* was carrying the Stanley Cup in Swift's purple track bag, then what were these kids about to reveal?

"You can't *take* that!" Isobel continued shouting. "How did you even—"

"The postman thought I was one of your brothers,

and he just put it down in front of us. Lucky me!" the mean one said with a smirk.

"Well, give it back. You can't take something that's not yours!" shouted Bond, taking a step toward them.

"Hand it over," added Edge, crossing his arms.

"Goodness, it's for *hockey*!" shouted Isobel. "It's not even *for* us—we were going to donate it!" She rushed toward them, but the boys had pulled the object out of the box and quickly snapped it away.

"A *hockey* trophy?" said the boy who was now holding Lord Stanley's shining silver bowl behind his back. "Well, in that case, maybe we should play for it!"

CHAPTER 11

The horses looked like they were on fire.

Lucas was hanging on to the edge of his seat—more a bench, really—as the horse-drawn buggy Isobel had him and his friends riding in slid and bounced and fish-tailed over the snow-covered grounds of Rideau Hall.

Ahead of them, Isobel's brothers, Edward and Arthur, were leading the way in a second buggy. They had with them one of their teammates from the Rideau Rebels, and two girls who'd been playing in Isobel's game on the rink. One of the girls, a secretary named Flo, worked in the government part of Rideau Hall; the other was Isobel's age.

The mean boys had told Isobel to get a team together and meet them at the Rideau Canal later that afternoon. And that's exactly what she and her friends were doing.

The air was crisp and cold. There was steam rising like smoke from the breath and haunches of the magnificent horses as they pulled the players along the streets toward the canal. This was why Lucas felt the animals were on fire. The buggy might have looked like part of a perfect wintery painting if they weren't going so quickly—racing to get this game over with so they could bring the cup home.

Isobel grabbed the reins and pulled on them, just as the man at the Montreal carnival had. "We're going to avoid the electric streetcars that they've just built on Rideau Street. The tracks are difficult for horses," she said, turning their buggy down some side streets and then onto Wellington Street, just as her brothers had done. "Soon, the railway will run all over Ottawa— but *I* will always have a preference for driving!" Isobel smiled as she snapped the reins against themselves and her horses moved even faster.

Edge, too, was holding on as tightly as he could. *We'll soon be clearing the snow off the biggest rink I've ever seen,* he thought excitedly. *If only Dadi could come to watch* this *game.*

Edge's family had travelled to Ottawa a few years ago, just after his grandparents moved from India to live with them. They'd taken a tour of the Parliament Buildings and skated on the Rideau Canal Skateway, the largest skating rink in the world.

Dadi had never skated before, so Edge's parents had rented her a sleigh to sit in on the ice. Edge had pushed it while skating, giggling as his grandmother had called it her Ferrari. Together, they'd covered the entire length of the skateway—7.8 kilometres from Dows Lake to the National Arts Centre. And then his parents had treated them all to a round of BeaverTails from a little stall on the side of the frozen canal. Edge's BeaverTail was a Killaloe Sunrise, and he'd licked his lips after each bite of the warm, deep-fried pastry with its thick coating of cinnamon and lemon juice.

"Look at that!" Bond yelled over the sound of the bells on the horses' harness straps. She was pointing toward the Parliament Buildings in the distance. "I kind of thought they'd be in black and white—like an old photograph." She'd tried to whisper this to Swift, but her words came out too loud.

"Uh, Isobel!" Edge shouted, trying to talk louder than the Chips' defender. He was using his big *acting* voice again. "Have you ever . . . *climbed* the Peace Tower?"

"Climbed the *what*?!" asked Isobel, confused.

As they passed in front of the government buildings, Edge quickly saw that his mistake was even worse than his teammate's. *There is no Peace Tower—not yet,* he thought, kicking himself.

What they were looking at in the middle of the Parliament Buildings was the Victoria Tower. It was a tall, skinny tower with many pointy parts and fine details. It looked like the top of a crown. The Victoria Tower would be destroyed in a fire in 1916—twenty-four years from now—along with the rest of the Centre Block (all except the library). What had burned would be rebuilt, but the tower would be changed. Edge had remembered this history from his family's trip to the capital, but here in 1892, none of it had happened yet.

Swift rolled her eyes. Bond shook her head. Edge, who was always looking out for everyone else, was the one spilling the beans about the future!

"Uh, Isobel—do you hear that?" Lucas asked desperately. The sound. The bells. *A distraction!*

Lucas quickly launched into a song, belting it out in time with the ring of the bells around the horses' necks.

Jingle bells, jingle bells,
Jingle all the way.
Oh! what fun it is to ride
In a one-horse open sleigh.
HEY!

The other Chips had all joined in for the "HEY!" but Isobel was blushing and laughing uncontrollably.

"You can't sing that song! That one is *not* for children!" she said, out of breath from all her giggling. Still, she pulled the reins and turned the buggy down a street to the left.

Swift looked at Lucas with her eyebrows raised. *Is she for real?*

"That is a song about *courting*—about taking a girl for a ride in a sleigh to make her fall in love with you!" said Isobel, as if this was a detail everyone should know.

Bond let out a loud "Ha!" before clapping her hand over her mouth. Lucas started blushing just like Isobel. Back in Riverton, they'd only ever thought the song was about bells! But Lucas didn't have any other ideas to get Isobel's mind off Edge's slip, so he continued all the way to the canal:

Dashing through the snow,
In a one-horse open sleigh,
O'er the fields we go,
Laughing all the way
HA! HA! HA!

*　*　*

The ten players were soon shovelling a rink that ran the width of the canal and was about twice that distance in length. It was rough work with their handmade shovels, giving Lucas a new appreciation for the wide metal snow shovel his parents had him use to clear the driveway. Soon, though, the group had what appeared to be a hockey rink. It even had low "boards"—snow piled high along the sides and ends, and packed tightly with the shovels.

Isobel's friends then spread out, gathering deadwood and the lower branches of spruce trees to make a bonfire later. They'd even brought a pot to boil some tea after the game. They set that down, along with the wood, beside a nearby ice-fishing shack.

Tea? Lucas thought. He didn't like tea. *Hot chocolate is so much better!*

When the mean boys arrived with only two friends of their own—a snivelling kid named Lloyd and one called John O'Brien, who'd been with their parents at Rideau Hall and was visiting from Renfrew—Edward and Isobel agreed to split the gang to make two teams of six skaters. It made sense: that's how the game was *always* played back then.

Isobel, Arthur, and Edward would be on the "Stanleys" team, fighting to take their cup back, and the two mean boys, Thomas and Henry (the meaner one), would be on the "Stealers" team with their buddies, trying to keep it.

"There's no extra players—no substitutes?" asked Bond, but no one seemed to know what she was talking about. A hockey game lasted an hour, Edward explained (as though she'd never played before), and all the players stayed on the ice the entire time.

"You'll have to be on the Stealers team with Lucas and Flo—to even it out," Edward continued, giving the two Chips and the Rideau Hall secretary an apologetic shrug.

"But no *trying* to lose," said Mean Henry, banging his stick on the ice. "And if I win that trophy, IT'S MINE TO KEEP!"

Flo rolled her eyes and crossed to the Stealers' side of the rink. Lucas and Bond reluctantly followed.

"Now what do we do?" Lucas whispered to Bond.

"He said we couldn't *try* to lose," said Bond, giving him a little jab with her elbow. "But that doesn't mean we have to score points."

Lucas swallowed hard as Isobel, across the ice, pulled out the black rubber disk she'd brought with her. *This could be my one chance to compete for the Stanley Cup*, thought Lucas, *and I've got to blow it? ON PURPOSE?!*

Swift tapped her stick against the two maple syrup buckets that would be her goalposts.

Edge looked across the ice at Lucas and Bond, and nodded. Then he slowly raised his hand behind his ear . . . and waved at them.

Nolan's sign for Bond from back in Riverton. But what does it mean HERE? Lucas had no idea.

And no time to think about it.

Edward had just put his two fingers into his mouth and blasted a whistle that would have stopped an NHL championship game in its tracks. "We'll play 'til the first team scores five goals!" he shouted into the wind.

Lucas giggled. What a funny game of shinny. At least there would be no shouts of *"CAR!"* because there was no such thing as cars in 1892.

And with that, Edward dropped the puck. "Game on!"

CHAPTER 12

Edge won the opening faceoff and accidentally sent the puck back to one of the Stealers. It was John O'Brien, the young kid from Renfrew who was playing the strange position of rover. Edge thought he seemed to be Mean Henry's cousin more than his friend, and he wasn't sure if they even liked each other. The kid went back toward Swift's net and then turned sharply and headed up ice. He was fast. Edge noticed right away and kicked himself into top gear as he gave chase.

The Chips' top scorer moved into full stride and felt the cold air on his face. His skates made a sizzling sound on the hard natural ice—a sound like when Dadi deep-fried samosas in a pan—and he could see that he was skating more quickly than the young puck carrier.

Just as John O'Brien crossed what would have been centre ice, had there been a red line, Edge came up alongside him and deftly used his stick to lift the other player's. The puck was now free, and Edge swept it away to begin stickhandling. But he didn't care for the feel of the short wooden stick Isobel had insisted he try. No sweet little curl at the tip of the toe—the old-fashioned stick was completely flat!

Mean Henry gave his friend Lloyd a push, and Lloyd started coming in hard to check Edge. Instinctively, the Chips' forward waited as he would have done back in Riverton, and at the last second, he tried to use his tuck play to pull Lloyd's stick out of position so that he could slide the puck between the Stealer's skates and be off.

Only it didn't work!

Using his wrists, Edge had flicked the stick handle to tuck the puck, but the puck had just kept going! Lloyd picked it up in full flight. He faked a forehand shot that Swift went for, deked around her, and lofted a backhand between the sap buckets and into the snowbank.

It was 1–0 for the Stealers.

Mean Henry skated over, smirking at Edge and Isobel. Lucas nodded in his best friend's direction, but all Edge did was give Nolan's wave again.

Let Bond get the puck, Edge was thinking as strongly as he could, staring at his friend. *She'll know what to do with it.*

If Edge's special move wasn't going to work, the Stanleys would need all the help they could get. That meant the Chips on the Stealers had to ditch the puck—grab it and not score with it. But Edge wasn't sure Lucas could do that. If his best friend couldn't even pass to Slapper in a practice, how would he stop himself from scoring in a game like *this*? Especially when the prize was the Stanley Cup!

It turned out that Edge was right.

Mean Henry won the next faceoff and sent the puck back to John O'Brien, who was deep in his own end.

Lucas, acting purely on instinct, saw his opening. With his feet moving in a blur, he took off straight up the ice, slamming his stick on the hard surface to get John O'Brien's attention.

The small kid from Renfrew saw what was happening. He fired a hard pass that looped over several Stanleys' sticks and landed perfectly on the blade of Lucas, who was now on a clear breakaway.

Edward's shrill whistle was like a shot being fired! *FFFF-rrrrrrlllllll!*

Then the whistle came again!

FFFF-rrrrrrlllllll!

Lucas could hear the others laughing. He stopped hard just as he reached Swift's net. With snow spraying out in front of him, he turned to see what had happened.

"Illegal pass," Edward sneered toward Lucas, wondering if he really *had* intended to score on their net. "No forward passing, lad."

These were the rules they'd been told in the beginning: six skaters on the ice, instead of five—that extra was a rover who could play wherever he was needed. And no forward passing allowed. *Ever.*

Lucas looked at Edge and finally understood. He couldn't be trusted—unless he gave up his obsession with scoring. Bond should be the one with the puck.

Luckily, John O'Brien had helped the Stanleys with that bad pass. *Had he meant to?* Edge wondered.

Lucas, of course, was thanking his lucky charm. *If this underwear can make goals, maybe it can also prevent them?*

Embarrassed and disappointed in himself, he gently kicked the puck toward centre for the next faceoff.

* * *

Gradually, the four Ice Chips adapted to the game as it was played by Isobel and her brothers. They stopped using forward passes and instead moved up the ice by having the puck carrier attract as many opposition checkers as possible—before dropping the puck back. The next player would then carry the puck as far as he or she could before dropping it again.

It was a game of two steps forward, one step back. Lucas couldn't believe what an incredible difference something as simple as the forward pass could make. It would transform the game into something far more exciting.

But *this* game was still fun. And Lucas was finally learning to let go of the puck!

After that, each time Lucas got the black disk, he passed it to Bond, who then pretended to lose it in her skirt, trip over it, or accidentally send it flying off into a snowbank. Luckily for Lucas and Edge, the Chips' defender was a far better actor than either of them.

Swift finally figured out how to do her adapted butterfly in her winter dress, and because she'd kept her own goalie stick (the one Isobel had offered her looked like the skinny ones for the outplayers), she'd been blocking shots left, right, and five-hole.

Soon, the score was 2–1 for the Stanleys, which had made Mean Henry's face grow red like a tomato.

Edge and Isobel had each scored one of those goals. And Isobel was playing as though she loved every single detail of the game. Nothing was above her and nothing was beneath her. She was a team player, just like Edge. It made sense that they'd found a rhythm together, dropping the puck to each other whenever they got stuck.

Isobel had just dropped the puck to Edge when he glided into a far corner that barely had a skate mark on it. It was like ice that had just been flooded. Lucas was right behind him, pretending he was going to snatch the puck away, when Edge's mouth suddenly dropped open.

There was a crack, then a splash.

And Edge was gone.

* * *

Swift couldn't believe how easily the ice had given way—how quickly Edge had disappeared! This was not a glitch—not a leap. This was way, way worse!

Lucas stopped instantly, snow spraying, and made to back away from the hole Edge had just created. He heard the ice under his own feet make a strange sound—a sort of moan—and then felt it go rubbery, flex down, and . . .

SNAP!

In an instant, Lucas, too, was under water.

Swift came skating as fast as her clumsy cricket pads would allow, but all who were rushing to the scene were held back by Isobel.

Edward let out a huge, desperate whistle—and everyone stopped.

"Don't go any closer!" he shouted. "That ice will never hold you!"

"*LUCAS!! EDGE!!*" Bond yelled, hoping to find out that her two friends had instead made a leap through time. *Maybe Crunch* did *fiddle with Scratch? Maybe he's called them home?*

The Stanleys and the Stealers were staring in shock. There were two holes in the ice where, moments earlier, there had been two hockey players. All that remained now was the puck, sitting alone between them.

"Look!" shouted John O'Brien, his face suddenly brightening.

Edge surfaced first, gasping and floundering in the freezing water. Then came Lucas, who was yelling, "*HHHHHELLLLLPPPPPPPPP!*"

Lucas felt like someone had run a cold spear through his heart and lungs. He was shouting, but he was also choking. His clothes weighed as much as an elephant. He tried grabbing the edge of the ice, but it broke off, making the hole even larger. He sputtered, choked, and went under again.

"They're *drowning!*" shouted a desperate Bond.

"Let's get them out of there!" yelled Swift, trying to skate toward the holes.

Isobel quickly grabbed her again. "No one skates there!" she commanded. "You have to spread your weight out so you don't go through."

Swift was stunned by Isobel's cool. She was taking charge.

"You boys," she said, pointing at Mean Henry and Thomas. "You get that fire going—*and fast!*"

The two Stealers looked terrified, but they quickly skated off in the direction of the unlit bonfire.

"Everyone else!" Isobel shouted. "Get down on the ice and crawl toward them in single file. Keep your sticks out in front of you. We'll hold on to each other's skates in case we get into trouble."

Edward went down on his belly and began wiggling toward the holes where Edge and Lucas had broken through. He kept his stick out in front, tapping and testing the ice as he went. It held.

Arthur was right behind, holding on to one of his brother's skates. Then Bond, then Swift.

Lucas surfaced again.

Isobel looked down at the other players on the ice. "Get your sticks to Arthur and Edward now! Move them up the line."

Each player began handing his or her stick to the player in front, who then moved it along to the next person. Soon Edward had eight sticks beside him on the ice.

Arthur quickly positioned four sticks into a square over each hole, and a moment later, Lucas and Edge were holding on to those sticks, rather than the ice. Nothing was breaking!

Edward reached over and grabbed Edge just above his wrists. The Chips' forward was shaking hard and his lips were blue—bluer than Lucas's, which is why Edward had gone for him first.

"Okay, everyone," Isobel called, still directing. "Start dragging the line back."

Slowly, almost like a sliver being pulled, Edge rose over the crossed sticks and, with a grunt, slipped onto more solid ice.

Then, with Edward's help and a gasp for air—for warmth—Lucas did the same.

CHAPTER 13

"You've got to get those wet clothes off or you'll DIE!" Isobel shouted as the players dragged the two frozen Ice Chips—now draped in the mean kids' winter coats—toward the bonfire.

"We're *f-fr-freezing*," mumbled Edge, barely able to move his arms enough to hold the coat over his body.

"No tea. I *hate* tea," Lucas stuttered, his teeth chattering, as he realized they were now beside the fishing shack.

The two mean kids—who still looked scared—had a fine fire going, the branches of the spruce trees snapping and sparking as they warmed the larger branches and sticks that had yet to catch. The flames were taller than a person, with sparks and smoke rising high into the sky.

"Get these boys some dry clothes!" Isobel shouted. The rest of the players looked in their bags and took off some of their extra layers. Soon, there was a small pile of clothes also being warmed by the fire.

"You need to change. *Now*," Edward said with concern in his voice. "Get those padded pants off. They're like sponges."

Swift and Bond were at their friends' sides, but they didn't quite know how to help them. Luckily, the Stanley children did.

"We've got big buffalo blankets in the buggies, but that won't be enough," said Isobel, calmly but sternly. "We've told you, if you don't get out of these wet clothes right now, you will freeze to death."

Lucas's heart was pounding and he was beginning to feel like he'd swallowed a dozen popsicles whole. He *was* freezing—from the inside out.

"I-I-I-I," he sputtered, unable to speak. The Chips' centre looked scared . . . and embarrassed. He was looking at the other Chips, his eyes pleading.

Swift immediately understood—so did Bond. The girls picked up some clothes from the pile and started leading their friends toward the ice-fishing shack a few metres away. They got the door opened just as Isobel arrived with the blankets.

"Edge and Lucas need a place to change—that's

away from the *wind*," Bond lied, trying to sound sure of herself.

"They'd better make it fast—then come back to the fire," Isobel said as the door closed behind them.

* * *

"*Th-that* was insane!" Lucas said when he finally got his voice back. He and Edge were alone in the ice shack, which was cold, but that time by the fire had already warmed them a little. Lucas's wet Ice Chips jersey was now lying on the floor and he had on an oversized sweater that Arthur had given him.

"Yeah, that was *awf-f-ful*," said Edge, shaking his head. "The *w-worst*!" He was trying to remember back to that time he'd gone skating on the canal with his family—a time when everything hadn't been scary and horrible . . . and freezing!

Neither the Stanleys nor the Stealers had any idea what would become of this canal in the future—that it would be opened to the public as a tourist attraction, beginning in the 1970s. Or that the canal's Winterlude festival would attract tens of thousands of daily visitors from around the world—people who'd come to marvel at the city's ice sculptures, drink hot chocolates, and skate together.

"We should have *t-tested* the ice," said Edge, thinking of how the modern canal would get checked every day for quality and thickness to make sure it was safe. "And we should have been more *c-careful*."

Lucas nodded as he fumbled with the laces at the top of his icy padded pants. The two friends had both found dry pants in the clothing pile; all they had to do was remove their wet ones and slip them on.

"I'm—I *can't* . . ." Edge started nervously. He reached for the laces on his own padded pants, but then he didn't undo them.

"Thank goodness the girls *b-brought* us in here!" said Lucas, changing his pants as quickly as he could. He was horrified just thinking about what could have happened if Isobel had made them change outside, in front of everyone. He imagined himself standing there for all to see, with the flames from the fire rising behind him, dressed in only his green underwear with its orange stars—inside out and backwards!

Then he pictured the mean boys, Isobel, her brothers . . . everyone laughing at him!

"*T-that* was a *c-close* call," said Edge as he picked

up one of the blankets and looked around nervously. He didn't want Lucas to see how embarrassed he was. He didn't want his best friend to know *why* he was waiting to change.

"Of course, it's probably our lucky *und-d-derwear* that saved us *f-from f-freezing*, right?" Lucas stuttered as he finished tying up his dry pants and started slipping on some warm socks.

Edge's face was even more flushed than it had been in the icy water; he looked panicked, frozen.

"I, uh—" he said, swallowing hard. He didn't want to lose his best friend, but he didn't want to die of hypothermia either.

"What are you waiting for?!" Lucas asked, worried. Edge had a strange look on his face—almost like he was going to cry. *Is he cold? Is he overheating? What is it?!*

"Can you . . . please *t-turn* around?" Edge said with a small voice. His teeth were still chattering and his eyes were wet with tears.

Lucas already had his back turned when he finally figured it out.

"You never turned your underwear inside out!"

* * *

"We should at least tell her *something*," Bond whispered to Swift as she stood by the fire, holding her hands out to warm them.

"We *can't*," Swift insisted, gently stepping on Bond's toes to tell her to keep her voice down. "We can't tell anyone about the future! What if they decide to change it?"

"We don't *know* that's how it works," said Lucas with a sympathetic shrug.

He and Edge had rejoined the kids around the fire, and the mean boys had taken back their coats and run off without a word. Isobel and her friends had barely noticed—everyone was feeling toasty and warm, relieved that the danger was gone. Lucky underwear or no lucky underwear, the two Ice Chips had survived their terrifying fall through the ice.

Feeling the burn of the fire on his face, the Chips' centre now found that he was thinking about Crunch—about Scratch's glitches, the players' strange little flip-flops through time, and the possibility that they'd *never* figure out time travel.

Crunch doesn't even know there are two Stanley Cups! he thought. But the idea made his brain hurt.

"Look, I wouldn't have the heart to tell Isobel that women's hockey won't grow at the same speed as men's—would you?" Swift continued, her face looking a little sad. Luckily, the fire was crackling so loudly that Isobel couldn't hear them.

"She's so excited about the game," said Edge, rubbing his hands together. "You can see how much she loves it—how much she wants to play."

"But then we could tell her the *rest* of the story!" said Bond, still annoyed that they had to keep all the good news to themselves. "Women's hockey *will* get better! And eventually, women will have their own leagues and their own awards. You know what I mean! The Clarkson Cup, and the—Isobel!" Bond swung her head toward the bonfire.

Isobel had been leaning down, placing a log on the other side of the fire, when she slipped on her long skirt—and fell!

"I'm fine, I'm fine," she said, getting up and dusting some soot off her hands. Luckily, she'd landed in an area where nothing was burning. The rocks were warm and had turned black with soot from an earlier fire, but that was all. "It's this silly dress," she said, holding up a piece of her skirt and leaving a sooty handprint behind. "But I guess we've *got to* wear them!"

"You won't *always* have to," called Bond as Swift gave her a little punch from behind.

"Maybe you should invent a *new* sport where girls don't wear long skirts," Edward said loudly, laughing at his sister. "Like swim jumping or horseback juggling or—"

"Or something bizarre like Naismith Ball!" said Arthur, joining in. "All you need is a football and two peach baskets!"

Edge was the first to figure out what they meant. When British people said "football," they meant soccer. And the peach baskets—it could only be . . .

This really is the beginning of everything! James Naismith—who grew up not far from here, in Almonte—had invented basketball in 1891!

"Have you *tried* this game?" Edge asked excited. The history of two sports in a single leap!

"No, but we met the man last year, just a few weeks after he invented it," said Edward. "He was back in town to visit his aunt and uncle. He thinks his little basket game will take off—but of course, one can never be sure."

"I think I'll stick to hockey either way, thank you kindly," said Isobel, giggling. She was trying to rub the handprint off her skirt but was only making it worse.

"You *should* stick with hockey—you're good," said a high-pitched voice, suddenly breaking into the conversation.

Outside the circle of warmth, Isobel turned to see John O'Brien, now with a knitted scarf folded in his arms.

"Hockey is a great game when it's played fairly," said the boy. "And it wasn't fair for my cousins to steal your cup."

The kid held the scarf out in front of him, and Isobel's eyes immediately brightened. Lucas, who now had Swift's purple track bag sitting at his feet, breathed a sigh of relief. The cup! With all the excitement, he'd almost forgotten about it.

John O'Brien handed the scarf to Isobel, and she immediately unwrapped it. Tears welled in her eyes when she saw that she was once again holding Lord Stanley's shining Dominion Hockey Challenge Cup in her hands!

"Thank you," Isobel said to the young kid.

"It's not from *me*," said John, blushing. He pointed

a little farther down the road, to where his cousins were waiting for him. "It's from *them*. They felt bad after your friends fell through the ice—they just didn't know how to say they were sorry."

"Well, I'm glad *you* were brave enough to give it back," Isobel said with a smile. She waved to the boys in the distance, and then turned her head toward her brothers. "Edward, Albert—can you take my friends back to the house in your buggy? Or wherever they need to go?" She'd begun gathering her things and was soon rushing back toward her own buggy. "Now that we've got the cup back, I have to get it somewhere safe. I'm not going to lose it again!"

Isobel had already climbed up onto the seat, grabbed the reins, and pointed her horse in the direction of Rideau Hall when Bond grabbed Swift's and Lucas's arms.

"But she *does* lose it," she said, her eyes wide and her voice a deathly whisper. "Did you see that soot mark on her dress from the fire? Isobel is about to *time-travel to Riverton*!"

CHAPTER 14

"You have to run FASTER!" Swift yelled at Edge and Lucas, waving her hand from the back of the electric train. The Chips had decided they didn't have time to wait for the Stanley brothers to put out the fire and collect their belongings. They had to get to Isobel and the cup. *Fast!*

With all her track training, Swift was the first to reach the streetcar, where she'd grabbed a railing at the back and leapt on. She'd pulled Bond up next, and now they were just waiting on Lucas and Edge.

But the train was picking up speed as it barrelled down Rideau Street, jostling the passengers, who were making their way home from work.

There should be a stop. There has to be a stop! Swift thought, but at the same time, she hoped the streetcar wouldn't stop at all. If they were going to catch Isobel

138

before the wormhole sent her to Riverton, they'd have to make it all the way to Rideau Hall.

Lucas pushed hard with his legs, like he would on a breakaway. He held the purple bag above his head and tossed it straight into Bond's outstretched arms—where it landed with a whump! His legs were burning, but he was so close that he and Swift could almost touch fingertips . . . until the train turned a slight corner and was gone!

"They'll find her," Edge said, huffing heavily. He'd stopped running and was now bent over with his hands on his knees. There was no way he and Lucas could have caught up to that train after their time in the frozen canal. They just didn't have enough energy!

"They'd *better* get to her before she leaps," said Lucas. "If Isobel loses the cup again, then what will we do? They'll be no Stanley Cup, no NHL . . ."

"I guess it's good that I started playing basketball, then," said Edge with a quick smile. "But here's what I don't get—why can't Swift just give her the cup in her bag?"

"How would she do *that*?" asked Lucas. "Hand it to her? Show her that there are two of them? Tell her we're here from the future to save the fate of the game?!"

A moment later, Edge was grabbing Lucas's arm and they were running again.

* * *

Swift and Bond arrived at Rideau Hall to find Isobel's horse still attached to the buggy, which was parked at an angle near the front doors.

"What do we do? *What do we DO?!*" asked Swift as she approached the doors and reached for the handle. Just as her hand was about to turn it, a man from the house—a butler or a driver—opened the door and let out a startled yell. He had a carrot in his hand for Isobel's horse, and he hadn't expected any visitors.

"We need to see Isobel!" Bond stammered, trying to sound like she was supposed to be there. "You *have* to let us in! We need to *stop* her!"

"Do you have an appointment?" the butler asked calmly, looking down his nose. Now that he was no longer startled, he wasn't about to be bullied.

"We just—" started Swift. She was clutching her track bag like it was her favourite stuffed animal. "We wanted to—" she tried again, but Bond was already holding on to the back of her jersey, pulling her away from the doors.

"Hey, don't worry about it, kind, uh, sir," said the Chips' defender, almost bowing as she slowly backed away. "We'll come back tomorrow. Thank you for your . . . uh, *hospitality*."

Once the butler had handed the carrot to the horse and closed the door behind him, Bond completely changed speeds.

"I know how this will work," she said quickly, looking at Swift with a new light in her eyes. "Give me your track bag."

Swift handed the bag over, but she had no idea what Bond had planned.

"What are you going to do with it?" she asked nervously.

"Just *trust me*," Bond whispered, looking around. "You take the front entrance, okay? I'm going around to the side of the indoor tennis courts. Do you remember when Lucas was talking about secret passages?"

"He *found* one?!" Swift asked, shocked.

"No," said Bond, swinging the track bag up on her shoulder. "But he did find a *back door*."

❋ ❋ ❋

Swift had finally, unexpectedly, worked her way into Rideau Hall, past the butler—her acting wasn't half bad, either—and she had climbed the stairs to the second level just in time to see the flash.

She'd spotted Isobel running down the hallway ahead of her, toward the display case, when she noticed the flicker. Anyone else would have just thought they'd blinked, but the time-travelling Ice Chips knew better.

There was a light—a bright one.

And then a scream . . .

And then the governor general's daughter was crashing down onto the carpet and hitting her head.

Isobel had leaped to Riverton—and then leaped back again!

"ISOBEL!" Swift yelled as she ran to her new friend's side.

Isobel's eyes were closed and she was moaning, saying something about being chased across the ice.

"It's okay," said Bond, appearing from behind a curtain. "It took her a while to find the keys for the display case, which made the timing perfect. Just let her wake up slowly. This is a tough one—don't you remember your very first leap?"

"I do," said Swift, wrinkling her nose. She was cradling Isobel's head in her hands and wiped some hair away from her eyes. "On that leap, I was completely turned around and confused. It took me a while to even figure out what had happened."

"That's *exactly* what I'm counting on," said Bond, smiling. She held up Swift's empty track bag and winked.

"Where am I?" Isobel asked, her eyes flickering. She reached her hands out beside her, searching for the bowl, but all she grabbed was air.

"You're at home, in Rideau Hall," Bond answered calmly. "You were putting the Dominion Cup in the display case, to keep it safe, when you tripped on a bump in the carpet."

Swift pulled on the carpet slightly, trying to make the bump look more pronounced.

"I tripped?" Isobel asked, her eyebrows twisted, as she finally opened her eyes. "But you were *there*," she said, looking at Bond. "And Edge! And Lucas! You had the cup. Where's the *cup*?! You were . . . *skating* toward me! Trying to take it?"

"Was *I* there? In your dream?" Swift asked, smiling as she helped Isobel to her feet. She knew full well that she'd been at her track practice in Riverton that day—and that this hadn't been a dream at all. But what else was she supposed to say?

"The cup is here? You mean the cup is *safe*?" Isobel asked, shaking her head and beginning to look more alert.

"It's *safe*," said Bond, pointing to where she'd just slipped the Chips' Dominion Cup—the one Edge had grabbed on the ice in Riverton. It was back in the display case, where it belonged.

"Oh, thank goodness!" said Isobel.

All three girls breathed a sigh of relief at exactly the same time.

CHAPTER 15

"You picked the lock?!" Lucas asked, laughing. Swift and Bond had buzzed the boys on their comm-bands, and the four had met up again at the lower end of Rideau Street.

"I picked *two* locks," said Bond proudly. "The back door *and* the display case. Crunch taught me how to do it at the Fix-it Club one night."

"Isobel never had to use her keys," Swift added with a smile.

While the girls were checking that Isobel was okay, they'd also gone over that strange "dream" she'd had, to make sure she believed that was *all* it had been. Their story was that she'd tripped on the carpet putting the cup into its display case, had a little dream about her friends, and then woken up to find the cup exactly where she'd left it.

Bond hadn't known how to explain *why* the two girls were in the house, since Isobel remembered leaving them at the rink, but Swift, as always, had been quick on her feet.

"Oh, but we forgot to give you back your dresses!" she'd said, grinning and offering one final awkward twirl. She then turned around and pointed to the buttons along her back. "Now that the game is over, can you *please* get me out of here?"

"Are you sure you don't want to keep them? I've got plenty," Isobel replied kindly, but the Chips insisted on changing into their old clothes. They'd leave the dresses at Rideau Hall, they said, in case some other girls wanted to try the game.

"This *is* your sport, just as John O'Brien said," Bond added as they prepared to leave. "You'll be able to switch from dresses in not too long. And soon—"

Swift had grabbed her arm to cut her off before she could say anything more.

Luckily, Isobel hadn't seemed to notice. "I know this is my game," she said, grinning. "And it's the greatest one on earth."

Now a light snow had started to fall, and the four Ice Chips realized they had no idea where they were going. They started to walk back up Rideau Street, toward the Parliament Buildings, but only because Edge had been talking about them again.

"You know what I'd love to see while we're here in Ottawa?" Edge asked, placing his hand, palm up, in front of him to catch some snowflakes.

"Summer!" Lucas answered and everyone laughed.

"At least it wouldn't be so bad if you fell in the water then," said Bond, wondering if it was too soon to make jokes about their fall through the ice.

"No, but it's true. It's the summer *logging* that I'd love to see here, in this time," said Edge, and everyone laughed again.

"Logging—like wood? Trees?" Swift asked, giving Edge a soft push on his shoulder.

"Well, yeah! Logs used to be floated down the river here, right behind the Parliament Buildings. Down the Chaudière Falls, too. The loggers made rafts out of the wood they had to move, and the workers even *rode* on them to move them around."

"Are you kidding? Where did you *learn* this stuff?" asked Bond, rolling her eyes and giggling.

"In Mr. Small's history class," said Edge, shaking his head. "Same place as you."

"I'm *not* riding a log down a river to travel back to Riverton," said Swift, pretending to balance on a floating piece of wood—and then pretending to fall.

"Of course you're not," said Edge, elbowing Lucas for a little help. "Once it gets dark, we'll sneak back to the outdoor rink at Rideau Hall . . ."

Lucas got the hint. "And then we'll strap on our skates . . . so we can glide home!"

* * *

"WE DID IT! YES!" Crunch cheered as the Chips came flying across the centre line of their ice back in Riverton with Swift's now empty purple track bag. "But where did you leave the bowl? Who did you give it to? Were you able to find that girl?"

"We found her—yes," said Lucas, slightly out of breath. "It all worked out. She has the cup. We saved the world—well, the hockey world."

"Ha! How did you save the hockey world?" asked Crunch, thinking Lucas was exaggerating. He was sitting in the stands with his tablet, in the same spot where Lucas and his friends had left him—hours earlier for the Chips, but only a moment ago from Crunch's perspective. "What kind of adventure were you on?" asked Crunch, moving toward the ice. "All you had to do was return that girl's salad bowl and get out of there!"

"Uh, Crunch, that wasn't a salad bowl," said Lucas, afraid to break the news.

"It *was* a silver cup—one that hockey players sometimes hold like *this*," said Edge, lifting his helmet over his head like he was cheering with a trophy. He was excited to see Crunch's reaction, but he wanted to make him guess. "They sometimes drink out of it, or take it to their hometowns to show it off."

"Or if you're Alexander Ovechkin, you take it swimming in a fountain," said Bond, getting tired of the suspense game.

"That bowl was the *Stanley Cup*, Crunch," said Swift, grinning. "And that girl was Isobel Stanley, the daughter of the man who donated the cup in the first place."

"So yeah, we saved the hockey world," said Lucas. "That is, if there's still a National Hockey League in this time. Did we do it? Did we save the Stanley Cup?"

Crunch's mouth was open, but not a single sound came out.

This was the weirdest landing back in Riverton that

the Chips had ever gone through. Normally, they were falling all over each other; this time, they'd just skated across the centre line like they were going for an evening skate along the canal. (Minus the freezing water holes.)

"How did that leap *feel*?" Crunch asked in the dressing room, when he was finally able to speak again. "I swear I didn't fiddle with anything." All four Chips were there, but he was looking at Bond and holding up his hands.

"The leap was . . . interesting," said Swift, thinking about how the wormhole had tossed them from scene to scene: the ice castle, the boy knitting the toque by the fire, and that time in the hospital, where they'd heard that baby's first scream.

"What do you mean?" asked Crunch, positioning his tablet so he was ready to take notes. "Were there glitches? Was this trip bumpier than usual?"

"We'll tell you tomorrow," Edge and Lucas answered at the very same time. The two Chips' forwards had never felt so tired. But they didn't know if that was because they'd fallen through the ice, run after an electric streetcar, or leapt through time. Or maybe it had to do with what awaited them in their own time:

The championship for the Golden Grail—the most important game of their lives.

CHAPTER 16

As Lucas and Edge approached the Blitz Sports Complex with their bags tossed up on their shoulders and their families following behind, they couldn't help feeling that this moment was a big one.

This was game day—the championship final. And it was the furthest the Ice Chips—*their* Ice Chips—had ever made it in a season.

By the end of this day, either the Riverton Ice Chips or the Riverton Stars would have their names added to their league's trophy, the Golden Grail. And the Chips knew that if *they* wanted to win it, they'd have to play better than they'd ever played before.

"LOOOOOOSERS!" Jared shouted as he and his sister breezed along the path toward the Stars' new high-tech arena *without* their equipment on their shoulders. Jared bumped Edge's bag and Beatrice bumped Lucas's. The two Stars didn't have their equipment with them because their father had probably arranged for one of his assistants to bring it. The Blitz twins were treated like royalty here at the Blitz Sports Complex—after all, it *was* their castle. Or at least, as Edge now called it, their Kingdom of Rinkness.

"Ignore them," said Edge, slowing down to wait for his grandmother, who'd called something to him in Punjabi. "Just think about your lucky underwear, *Top Shelf-eroni.* Think about how you'll feel when that lucky underwear kicks those nasty Stars' butts!"

Lucas smiled. He knew his linemate thought his superstitions were ridiculous, but he was still nice about them. If Lucas forgot to do part of his lucky routine—like kissing his fingers and touching the trophy case or rubbing his quarter—Edge was always there to remind him. Edge wanted Lucas to be the best Lucas he could be. *That* was what friendship meant to him.

"Have a *gooooood* game," Edge's dadi said to Lucas once she'd caught up. "And pass that rubber tiki!" This was the most English Lucas had ever heard her say. She didn't speak it much, even though Edge always told him that she understood the language very well. Lucas loved that she called their puck a "tiki," after an Indian dish made of potatoes.

"Wait, where's your jersey?" Lucas asked her. Dadi was wearing the same kind of clothes she normally wore to their games, but she had a light beige cardigan over top, rather than her lucky hockey jersey.

"Edge's dada has it in his backpack," she said, continuing in English as they walked toward the rink. "New superstition—you will like it. Once his grandfather has parked his Ferraris, I will show you."

*   *   *

In the dressing room—on this big, amazing day—Lucas didn't care *who* saw that his bright red underwear was on inside out and backwards. In fact, he *wanted* his teammates to know that he was going to be lucky that afternoon, and that out there on the ice, his luck would be working its hardest.

"Hold on—your grandfather has a Ferrari? And more than one of them?" Lucas asked Edge, surprised, as he pulled his socks on over his shin pads. There was so much talking in the dressing room, so much excitement, that he almost needed to shout.

"No, *no!*" Edge said loudly, laughing. "He has two *crutches* that he's supposed to use while his broken knee heals. My grandmother's been calling them his Ferraris to make them sound cooler—to make sure he uses them. It was either that or the names of two wrestlers."

"That's great that he's here, too," said Swift, who was dressed and ready to step onto the ice. Her parents were in the stands. And of course, her sister, Sadie—"Blades" to the Chips—would be playing in the game with the rest of the team.

"I think *everyone's* here," said Slapper, who'd walked over while tucking in one side of his jersey, which was the way he always wore it. "My dad took the day off from his construction job, too. Man, this is so exciting! I've even—"

Slapper suddenly had a worried look—and it was directed at Lucas.

"You've got your underwear on backwards, am I right?" Lucas asked, his eyebrows raised. When Slapper nodded yes, Lucas smiled sympathetically and patted his teammate on the back. "Good. You're going to do well out there—and we'll need all the luck we can get!"

The dressing room was starting to sound like a symphony of mismatched instruments: Swift and Bond were laughing loudly (maybe about what it would be like to wear dresses for *this* game); Lars was sitting on a bench, bouncing his knees up and down; Blades was tapping her stick; and Crunch and Mouth Guard were passing a roll of tape back and forth with their sticks. *Click. Click. Click.*

There was a rhythm to their dressing room. A beat. And definitely a lot of nervous energy.

"Put your hands on your shoulders if you can hear me," Coach Small said in his quiet way as he walked into the noisy dressing room, tapping his pen against the top of his clipboard.

A few Chips put their hands on their shoulders, but many just continued on the way they were.

"Put your hands on your knees if you can hear me," Coach Small continued as more joined in. "Put your finger on your nose if you can hear me."

Almost every Chip now had a finger on his or her nose—all except Mouth Guard, who had his finger *in* his nose, as usual.

Looking around the room, Edge thought about how each of his teammates was different. Crunch was brainy, Bond was strong, and Mouth Guard always said what he thought—even when he wasn't thinking at all. Swift was determined. Blades took risks. Dynamo was quiet. And Lucas put in more effort than any of them, regardless of the state of his equipment. No two Ice Chips were the same, but they were all where they belonged. This was *their* team. This was *their* home. This was *their* family.

See, hockey is for everyone, Edge thought as he quietly listened to Coach Small's pep talk. Then he put on his helmet and followed the rest of his teammates out toward the rink.

✳ ✳ ✳

"Tell Lucas this is for him—for *our team*," Dadi told Edge as she leaned over the boards while the players were filing in. She was now wearing her jersey—as were her husband, Edge's parents, and his little sister, Noor— and she was holding a kohl pencil in her hands.

Dadi knew that Lucas would be at the end of the line—another one of his superstitions—but she also knew that the two linemates would be together on the ice.

Edge looked up and chuckled. Then he turned his head so his grandmother could draw a black dot behind his ear, as she'd often done to Noor.

"For luck," she said with a smile and a pat. "*Mahriaa shot, keeta goal!*"

And then she turned to go back to her seat.

"What on earth is that?" asked the Face, who'd been walking behind Edge.

"She thinks it's bad luck to be perfect," said the Chips' top scorer, grinning. "If I have a mark like this—something that makes me not perfect—she thinks I'll play a perfect game."

* * *

The light show that filled the arena to kick off the match was absolutely insane. No wonder it had taken days to complete.

The moment the Zamboni finished clearing the ice, the rink lights dimmed and the music, sounding more like it belonged in Cirque du Soleil than a novice hockey game, hit full volume.

A bright white light banged on, shining down onto the red centre line. A player then appeared on the ice—suddenly, even though no door had opened in the boards.

"Oh, goodness, it's a hologram," Swift said to Lucas, rolling her eyes.

Both she and Lucas were standing with their helmets pressed up to the glass—Swift with her regular goalie helmet, and Lucas with the second-hand one he'd just bought with the allowance he'd saved. It smelled better than Speedy's old helmet—the one he'd lost on their leap—but the sizing was still wrong. Luckily, his parents hadn't even noticed the change.

This 3D hockey player who'd been created with beams of light was skating around the ice with his arms over his head, and both Lucas and Swift felt a shiver. It was like he was taunting them.

"This isn't just a *hologram*—it's a hologram of *Jared*," Lucas said, squinting. *Of course it's a Blitz.*

Next a hologram of Beatrice lit up, and then, one by one, images of their teammates appeared in flashes. The fake Stars began whirling around the rink like a cyclone gathering energy, distracting the spectators while the *real* players filed in toward the centre. By the time the announcer had called the last player's name and number, they were all huddled at centre ice, in the

middle of the cyclone . . . waiting. The bright white light's circle on the ice grew just big enough to include all the Stars players—the real ones.

The holograms were gone.

That's when Coach Blitz worked his way into the middle of the group and started shouting.

After each rough, angry call, his players were there to answer him:

"WHO BURNS BRIGHTEST?!"

"THE STARS!"

"WHO BURNS BRIGHTEST?!"

"THE STARS!"

"AND WHO'S ON FIRE?"

"WE ARE!"

"WHO'S ON FIRE?"

"WE ARE!"

"NOW LET'S BURN UP THE ICE. I SAID, 'BURN UP THE ICE'! LET ME HEAR YOU!"

"STARS! STARS! STARS!"

"STAAAAAARS!"

This was the Coach Blitz's new cheer, and Lucas hated it—all the Ice Chips did. They also hated the fact that they had no cheer to send back at them.

"We never came up with anything," said Edge,

bumping Lucas's arm with his stick. "Coach Small said we could make up our own cheer, but we didn't. We forgot."

"We were too busy leaping, and now it's too late!" said Bond, disappointed. They all watched as the Stars moved over to their half of the ice, with Jared and Beatrice acting like they'd just been crowned.

The regular lights came back on, and soon the announcer was talking again, calling out the Ice Chips' numbers and names. Only now, it was as though he was too bored to be there.

"Number 17, Ekamjeet Singh . . ."

"Number 8, Tianna Foster . . ."

CHAPTER 17

FRRRRRL-FWEEET!

The referee's whistle blew, calling Lucas and Beatrice to centre for the faceoff.

"We looked in your stinky purple gym bag," Beatrice said with a sneer as she leaned forward and placed the heel of her stick on the ice in front of her. "Nice *fake trophy*. You guys really *are* losers."

"Why do *you* care?" Lucas sneered back. In his head, of course, he was thinking about the Stanley Cup, and about the fact that he—Lucas "Top Shelf" Finnigan—had actually, finally, had the chance to hold it above his head. It didn't matter that it was in Swift's purple bag at the time, or that he wasn't skating but running to catch an electric streetcar.

What was important was that he'd held it. Seen it. Smelled it.

And that had taught him something he'd never expected to learn.

He *wanted* to hold a trophy over his head, but that trophy wasn't the Stanley Cup. His dream was to do what he was doing at this very moment: fighting for the right to hoist the Golden Grail, just as the Ice Chips had done in that old photo he loved so much.

"Well, I *don't* care if you're losers," Beatrice said awkwardly—it was the only comeback she had. That and sticking out her tongue.

Lucas just rolled his eyes. The Blitz twins never changed, not even for a championship match.

FFFF-RRRRRRLLLLLL!

The referee blew his whistle again, and the round black disk was dropped to the ice.

They were off!

Beatrice won the first faceoff and sent the puck flying into the curve of Jared's stick, where it landed without a sound. Jared stickhandled twice, but then surprisingly went for a slapshot on the Chips' net, probably trying to show off for the crowd. The puck didn't even make it to Swift, and Bond picked it up easily, sending it around the boards behind their net.

The Stars' fans jumped to their feet anyway, some

of them even cheering. Lucas's parents clapped and yelled, "Go, Ice Chips!" a couple of times. But Edge's dadi didn't say a thing.

Lucas won the next faceoff and got the puck back to Edge, who was ready for it. He smiled—he'd been practising his tuck move all morning, to make sure he still had it.

Jared was now barrelling toward him, but Edge saw him coming and waited until the very last moment before trying his special play. Once the Stars' forward was on him, Edge used the tip of his stick to flip the puck back and draw it toward himself. Then once Jared reached for it, Edge slipped it through his opponent's skates and was off and running!

"HEY!" Jared called out as he turned to go after Edge, but Beatrice, appearing to misread her brother, suddenly plowed into him. The Blitz twins were flat on their backs on the ice when Edge went five-hole on the Stars' goalie, easily slamming the puck into the back of the net.

It was 1–0 for the Ice Chips. They were one point closer to their trophy!

Edge circled around and offered Jared his hand. "Sorry about that," he said, grinning. When Jared didn't take the hand and scowled, he added: "I guess she thought you were a hologram."

Edge's grandfather was the first up on his feet and cheering, but Edge's grandmother still hadn't moved. She was looking at the Stars' coach, and she was frowning.

"*MAAAHRIAA SHOT! KEEEETA GOAL!*" was soon ringing out across the arena, but Edge wasn't sure who had even started it. The rest of the Chips' fans were jumping to their feet, and the Stars' fans had started booing.

"This seems too easy," Lucas whispered to Edge. He couldn't understand why the Stars were playing so badly.

Jared Blitz hates that tuck play. Does he never see it coming?

* * *

"Great move, Edge," Coach Small said, slapping the Chips' top scorer on the back after his second goal—scored using his special play.

They were nearing the end of the first period when Nolan went for the puck, but Beatrice stole it from him . . . and fumbled it. Jared then lazily picked up the rebound off the boards and sent a saucer pass into the middle of nowhere. None of the Chips knew why.

It was 2–0 for the Ice Chips when the buzzer went, signalling the end of the period. Lucas didn't get it. *Are the Stars actually trying to lose? Or are they working on a plan?*

The announcer was asking everyone to clear the ice to make room for a flood—there would be three this game—and of course, another light show.

Lucas was on his bench, watching the various Stars' players file off the ice, when he finally made eye contact with Nolan.

The Stars' defenceman pulled off his helmet and mouthed something, but Lucas couldn't make it out— he was too far away. Next, Nolan made a sign with his gloves still on, pointing his fingers like he was about to shoot, then dropping one "gun" down on top of the other. Lucas still didn't get it. He turned to take a sip from his water bottle and saw that Shayna, Nolan's sister, had skated back onto the ice to pick up a glove she'd dropped near the Chips' bench.

"It's the underdog thing," Shayna explained as quickly as she could out of the side of her mouth. "You

guys get all the cheers because no one expects you to win—and then sometimes you do."

Lucas nodded. He kind of understood.

"We *want that*—Coach Blitz *wants that*. We're tricking you," Shayna continued. "The plan is: you win the first period, and then we'll kick your butts for the rest of the game. That's how everyone will love the Stars." A moment later, Shayna was stepping off the ice with the rest of her team.

* * *

Slapper squished himself between Edge and Lucas, who were waiting near the boards as the next light display was beginning.

"We're doing awesome," he said, wrapping an arm around each of his teammates and giving them a little squeeze.

The Chips had walked back to their dressing room to retape or wipe their hair with towels, but as usual, Coach Blitz had insisted that they return to watch the show he'd prepared.

"It's a trick, Slapper," Lucas said loudly once the music had started.

As the lights changed, cracks and holes appeared on the ice—they were projected like the holograms—and the sound of snapping ice went crackling through the arena. A moment later, pieces of the ice seemed to fall away, leaving behind gaping holes of lava.

"If they add holograms of *us* to this, I'm leaving," Edge said, feeling a little shiver go down his spine.

Then in a flash, the entire ice surface was a chessboard, and holographic Beatrices and Jareds were appearing on different squares.

"How is it a trick?" Slapper asked, looking hurt. "You mean we're not really this good?"

"We could be—we *can* be," said Lucas, thinking about what he'd learned in their half-ice practice, and then what he'd learned about himself out on that frozen canal. "We can do this," he said, tapping Slapper's stick with his own. "But *you'd* better be ready to score."

Slapper stared straight ahead at the bizarrely lit ice and swallowed hard.

CHAPTER 18

"Those lights are so *weird*," the Face said to Edge and Swift as the Chips all filed back onto the ice to make a loop before beginning the second period. "Edge, you're lucky you're getting to score so much. Your grandma must be going wild."

Edge shrugged his shoulders. He was never sure what the Face was really saying. Half the time he was bragging, and the other half he was just confusing.

"It's tough out there today," Swift said to the Face, banging her stick against his pads. "But hopefully you'll get a chance in net, too." Because Swift was so good, the Face barely got any ice time—and Swift never let herself forget that.

The three Chips looked up as the Stars' cheer started at the other end of the rink. This time, it was so loud it sounded like they might even be using the announcer's microphone:

"WHO BURNS BRIGHTEST?!"

"THE STARS!"

"WHO BURNS BRIGHTEST?!"

"THE STARS!"

"AND WHO'S ON FIRE?"

"WE ARE!"

"We *really* need a cheer," Lucas said to Edge as his friend caught up with him on the ice. "If the Stars are trying to trick us—and trying to psych us out—we need to fight back in every way we can."

* * *

Lucas took the next faceoff, and the puck went back to Edge and then back to Lucas again. Both Blitz twins were speeding toward Lucas when he tried Edge's tuck play, but he was too slow. Beatrice poke-checked him and the puck was soon rattling around in the Chips' end again.

Beatrice quickly roofed a wrister for the Stars' first goal, and then when Lucas lost the next faceoff, Jared got them with a slapshot that slipped past a gap in Swift's pads and was in.

The game was tied 2–2 at the end of the second period. But Lucas could tell that the Blitz team was just getting started—they *really were* about to crush them.

* * *

"Okay, I'll do it," Slapper said, almost whispering into his jersey. He'd walked over to Lucas and Swift in the dressing room—it was their last break before the final period. "Just don't make me look like a dummy in front of my dad. Don't steal my puck again."

"*Wooo!* The Stars are *shining* tonight!" Jared shouted in the hallway as Mouth Guard, who was playing with the Chips' dressing room door, swung it open and shut again. The next time it opened, Jared blew a kiss to the Chips, which made the players furious.

"Oh, yeah?" Lucas yelled back, puffing out his chest. "Well, I hope you brought your *sunglasses* tonight. Because our *whole team* is stellar!"

"Yeah—and we're about to go supernova!" Edge added, laughing.

"You guys are weak," said Bond, giggling. "Now what's our cheer?"

"We don't have one," said Mouth Guard, still at the door.

"Well, let's change that!" demanded Dynamo. His knees were already twitching; he was ready to get back on the ice.

"Change that how?" asked Lars, as though he didn't believe it could be done.

"What about saying ice is *cool*—you know, like chillin'," suggested Slapper. He was trying his best.

"How about . . . no, nothing. Forget it," said Crunch.

"A *song* about ice? Are we allowed to sing a song?" asked Bond, looking hopeful.

Lucas shook his head. Edge's brain was starting to hurt.

"Um, I think *I* know what we want," said the Face, clearing his throat and stepping forward. For once, he didn't sound full of himself. "It's perfect, I promise. But I should ask first. I want to make sure we're allowed."

The Face had the most serious expression the Chips had ever seen.

And he was looking directly at Edge.

* * *

The final light show had something to do with butter-
flies being released into space, and a hockey player who
looked like Coach Blitz skating around a tiny planet like
he was the Little Prince on ice. Lucas couldn't imagine
how anyone had understood it, but still the Stars' fans
had cheered wildly.

"Everyone squeeze in, gather together," Swift said
once the Chips had made their loop of the ice. They
squished themselves into a small circle in their own
end and put their arms over one another's shoulders,
just as their opponents were doing.

The Stars were the first to launch their cheer:

"WHO BURNS BRIGHTEST?!"

"THE STARS!"

"WHO BURNS BRIGHTEST?!"

"THE STARS!"

Then it was the Chips' turn.

"Are you sure?" the Face asked Edge one final time
as he wiggled his way into the centre of the group.

"It's a *great* idea," said Edge, his heart suddenly
feeling full.

So the Face, the kid who always wanted the

attention—*any* attention—on him, opened his mouth and yelled:

"*MAAAAAAHRIAA SHOT!*"

"*KEETA GOAL!*" the rest of the Ice Chips answered at the top of their lungs.

"*MAAAAAAHRIAA SHOT!*"

"*KEETA GOAL!*"

"*MAAAAAAHRIAA SHOT!*"

"*KEETA GOAL!!!*"

Then Lucas, the team captain, took over:

"WHO OWNS THE RUBBER TIKI?"

"WE DO!"

"WHOOOO OWNS IT?"

"WE DO!"

"WHO OWNS IT?"

"WE DO!"

"GOOOOOOO, RIVERTON ICE CHIPS!!"

The Face's cheeks were red from all the shouting. He was smiling—almost glowing. The Chips' second goalie, probably the only person on the team who'd never scored a goal or had an assist, had just taken Edge's grandmother's special call . . . and roofed it.

CHAPTER 19

Lucas didn't even use the gate when it was time for the next line change. He was so eager to get back onto the ice that he leapt over the boards.

The Chips were changing on the fly. Slapper was already out and Lucas took a pass from Mouth Guard, who was heading for the bench so Edge could get on.

At the same time, the Blitz twins were coming onto the ice from the Stars' bench, with Beatrice skating fast toward Lucas.

Lucas held the puck, and then passed it to Edge a second after his friend's skates touched the ice.

Jared was on Lucas like a nasty mosquito—a mosquito with elbows—but once the puck had been passed, the mean Star turned and went after Edge.

The Chips' forward used his tuck move on Jared, and it worked—again! *Maybe this is why Jared booed so loudly when I used this move on the Orcas? He's got nothing to counter it!* Edge smiled to himself as he used the same trick on the Stars' goalie, who practically left him an open net on which to shoot.

It was 3–2 for the Chips! They were winning again!

Edge's teammates piled onto him, and the cheering from the crowd quickly turned into a roar.

There was one voice, however, that was louder than all of them. And Edge was proud to pick it out.

"MAHRIAA SHOT, KEETA GOAL!!!"

"Beauty," Lucas said to his friend once the players were moving back into position.

"Slapper" was all Edge said back, but he was smiling. He was hopeful.

"I know," said Lucas, glancing up to the corner where Slapper's dad was sitting, wearing his usual Montreal Canadiens hat. And waiting.

The next goal went to Beatrice, tying the game at 3–3. It had slipped so easily through Swift's five-hole that the Chips' goalie immediately skated over to the bench.

"Put the Face in," she said to Coach Small. "I'm getting tired—give Matías a turn."

"Are you sure?" the coach asked. When Swift nodded, he called out: "Rodriguez, you're up!"

Swift could have sworn the Face had tears in his eyes when he turned.

Despite the goal she'd just scored, Beatrice gave Edge a sour look when she showed up to take the next faceoff against him. The puck was dropped and she plucked it out of the air, right in front of him, then sent it back to her brother.

"This is it—you're done!" Jared yelled at the Chips, loud enough for the entire rink to hear him. He was smiling like a firefighter who'd just saved a dog from a burning building, but he hadn't done anything of the sort. He'd cheated, he'd played nasty—as usual, Jared had been a jerk.

The game is tied and we're about to go into over-time, thought Lucas. *But that doesn't mean that any of this is over.*

Mouth Guard was scrambling to get back out and into the play when Jared shot the puck back to Beatrice. She lunged for it, hoping for a hat trick, but Mouth Guard had already snapped it up and passed it on.

Now Lucas had the black disk, and Slapper was in perfect position.

A quiet *"Mahriaa shot, keeta goal!"* sounded in the stands, as the big bear of a defenceman smiled.

Lucas's pass was still spinning across the ice when Slapper's stick smacked down right on top of it with a clack! The onlookers gasped when they realized that this young player had just slapped the puck harder than they'd ever seen in a novice game—with the force of Zdeno Chara.

It was a beautiful goal—the sort of goal Slapper, with his great one-timer, should have been scoring every game. And it had happened at the very last second, just before the final period had timed out and the buzzer sounded.

"*MAHRIAA SHOT, KEETA GOAL!!!*" the fans on the Chips' side all yelled as they quickly jumped to their feet. Slapper, grinning up at his dad as he rounded the ice, spun his stick into the position of an air guitar, got down on one knee . . . and *played*.

The game was over.

The horn had blown.

And the Riverton Chips had won the championship!

Lucas and his teammates gathered around Slapper, piling on top of him to congratulate him on such a spectacular shot—on their win!

Now, thought Lucas, staring at Jared's and

Beatrice's grumpy faces from the pile of players he'd landed in. *Now, you can say it's over.*

* * *

"My hair smells like strawberry ice cream," said Mouth Guard, nudging Crunch annoyingly, and then nudging him again. He was uncomfortable waiting in line to accept his medal. And he wasn't the only one. The Stars were angry, and many of them felt cheated out of the trophy they thought they should have won. The Chips, however, exhausted from playing their hearts out, were blushing all the way down the line. They were excited about their success, but they were also nervous about the completely over-the-top Blitz-style celebration that had already begun.

In the days leading up to this match, Coach Blitz had designed the winner's celebration, just as he had the arena's light displays—all of it with the Stars in mind.

It was wild—like nothing anyone in Riverton had ever seen before.

A red carpet had been rolled onto the ice, followed by a gold-coloured Cadillac—for the winning coach to sit in. If Coach Blitz's team had won, he would have jumped into it right away and probably honked the horn through the entire ceremony, but George Small was just standing by the car, wearing his old baseball cap and smiling. He was happy his team had won—proud of them—but there was no way he was getting in.

The sound system was playing music loudly, but it also had sound effects going. There was a screeching noise when the Cadillac rolled out, and when the podium was set up, it made sounds like huge metal blocks being moved in a video game.

"Luckily, I *love* strawberry ice cream," Mouth Guard said, smiling, as Mayor Abigail Ward walked past him and stepped up to the podium.

"The Riverton Ice Chips have had a long road to get here," she started, turning and giving Lucas, Edge, and Swift a wink—she hadn't forgotten that this was their dream. "At the beginning of the season, they didn't even have a rink. But they fixed that, and then worked their hardest out on that ice."

Jared moaned and Beatrice rolled her eyes, shifting on her skates. They'd worked hard, too, they probably thought. And they most definitely thought they deserved this more than the Chips.

"I'll give out the medals first," the mayor said as four gold trays full of medals were walked onto the ice. "And then Coach Blitz has prepared something special for the trophy presentation."

Mayor Ward started with the silver medals on the left side of the podium, placing one over the head of each Star. Nolan and Shayna smiled when they accepted theirs—a silver was still a great accomplishment—but many of the other Stars sneered or giggled, unable to hide their disappointment.

Next, the mayor moved on to the Chips.

"Number 12, Sebastián Strong," the announcer said into his wireless microphone as he walked along behind the mayor. "Number 21, Dylan Chung."

The mayor stepped up to Crunch and put a gold medal around his neck, and then she did the same to Mouth Guard, Bond, and Slapper, who couldn't stop smiling.

"Do you think we can get little stickers shaped like medals, to stick onto our hockey cards? I've already signed mine," Slapper asked eagerly. But the mayor was already farther down the line. She was placing a medal around Blades, then Lars, then Dynamo, then the Face, then Edge . . .

"I have no idea what Coach Blitz has planned," the mayor said as she put a medal around Lucas's neck, then Swift's. "But I hope you're ready to lift that Golden Grail up over your heads—you all deserve it. I *know* that you've put in a lot of extra practice." She winked after this last sentence, which made Lucas wonder if she knew about the practice they'd been getting *outside* of Riverton, with the help of some of hockey's greatest stars. *Does she know we've been leaping?*

When it was time for the Golden Grail to appear, Lucas couldn't believe how nervous he felt.

Coach Blitz's light show projected a bunch of balloons on the ice, and then had them break apart and sail up into the rafters. When they reached the top, the small light creations exploded, sending fake holographic confetti onto the heads of everyone on the ice below.

That's when the hockey holograms returned.

First it was Beatrice, then Jared. They were holding a hologram of the novice trophy above their heads as they skated around the ice.

"Just bear with me," said Coach Blitz as he coughed and leaned in to the microphone on the podium. "Obviously, we thought the game would go another way—but my guys look good, don't they?"

The Blitz twins' holograms evaporated as the lights slowly dimmed. Mayor Ward and her father, Quiet Dave, disappeared into the Zamboni chute, and when they came back, there were carrying the Golden Grail on a golden platter. Lucas actually gasped. It was the most beautiful sight he'd ever seen.

"Ladies and gentlemen, the winners of this year's Golden Grail trophy are . . . South Riverton's Ice Chips!!" the announcer yelled, finally sounding enthusiastic about their team.

The mayor stood in front of Lucas with the platter, but it took a few moments for him to get what she was doing.

"Will you take it?" she asked, grinning as the entire audience looked on—waiting. "We'll need a new picture for your trophy case."

With the sound of cheers and applause in the background, Lucas reached over and took the Golden Grail with the help of his two best friends.

Once Lucas, Edge, and Swift had the trophy hoisted over their heads, the flash of a camera went off, leaving everyone blinking.

CHAPTER 20

The black basketball bounced off the Plexiglas at the back of the net and went through the hoop with a whoosh.

"I bet you can't keep going," said Lucas. He was making fun of Edge, trying to see how many times in a row his best friend could sink a shot, but he was also quite impressed. The basketball practice Edge and his dad had been doing for the past couple of weeks was really paying off. Edge was already up to twelve!

"How's your *Naismith* Game?" Bond asked, giggling, as she steered her skateboard onto the basketball court at Riverton Public School—the place where Edge and Lucas had told all the leaping Chips to meet. She snapped her board up into her hands before resting it against the picnic table.

"I'll tell you in a minute," Edge said with a grin. "Just let me get it in the peach basket a few more times first." He tossed the ball up against the backboard and into the net, grabbed the rebound, and did it again.

"Lucky shot! You must have put your underwear on backwards this morning," Swift joked from the picnic table, where she was sitting with Crunch and reading about the Chips' gold medal win on his tablet. The story said that the mayor was proud of them. That the town was proud of them. And that winning the Golden Grail had meant everything to the team.

"Dadi doesn't believe in Top Shelf's underwear trick," Edge said with a laugh as he went for a layup and sunk that, too. "But she does think it's funny."

At the end of the trophy ceremony, all of the Chips' friends and family members had joined them in a large conference hall at the side of the Blitz arena. They'd had cups of juice and tiny fancy sandwiches—all stamped with the Stars' logo, all from Coach Blitz's original plan. Everyone had had a great time, not just because of the win, but also because they were all together.

It was one of the biggest parties the town of Riverton had ever seen.

That's when the Face had explained that he'd always wanted to be an outplayer, scoring goals, but had decided to play net because he had asthma like

Jacques Plante, the first goalie to wear a mask in a regular game (and a French Canadian who'd knitted his own toques as a kid!).

That was also when Swift's parents had presented their daughters with the pack of movie tickets they'd promised if they won, joking that their next trophy would get them each a gold Cadillac like the one on the ice.

"Maybe if it's the Stanley Cup," Blades had answered, laughing. "Or the Isobel Cup—that's the one Swift wants to win!"

Swift's cheeks turned red and tears began to well up in her eyes. She was thinking about their latest leap: how she'd held the Stanley Cup and met Isobel Stanley, for whom the championship trophy of the National Women's Hockey League was named. Isobel, the goalie had since learned, had married—changing her name to Isobel Gathorne-Hardy—and had been gone for a few decades by the time the cup was created in 2016. Her spirit, however, had definitely remained.

At one point, Slapper's dad had come over to where Lucas and his friends were dipping strawberries in a chocolate fountain, and he'd given his son a

big, awkward hug. Then he'd given hugs to Lucas and Edge, too, for the assist.

"He's no Walter Gretzky," Slapper had said with a shrug when his dad left to get a sandwich. He was talking about how Wayne Gretzky's dad had played such a big role in his son's hockey career—he'd probably been to every game and every practice. "But I do love the big guy."

Slapper, finally feeling like he was back in with his friends, had told his teammates that he'd basically been born a fan of the Montreal Canadiens. His father was a fan, and his father's father. And his great-great-uncle was the guy who'd started the team—John Ambrose O'Brien, from Renfrew.

"John O'Brien's the same guy who got rid of the rover position," Slapper's dad had added, his mouth full. He wasn't expecting any of the Chips to know what he was talking about, but of course, the ones who'd been to Ottawa in 1892 would never forget that kid.

Near the end of the night, Coach Small had made the shortest speech ever, saying only, "Thanks to all of you for a great season. Congratulations!"

And then Edge had grabbed the mic and shouted: "Hey, South Riverton, enjoy this moment and have fun with it!" just like Kawhi Leonard had after the Toronto Raptors won the NBA final in 2019.

Edge and Lucas went home with their families—with Dadi wearing Edge's medal—but then the two of them had talked on their comm-bands late into the night. They'd never been so happy.

* * *

"I forgot to thank your grandmother for our win," said Lucas, grabbing Edge's rebound and going for his own shot—a toilet bowl that rolled around the rim for what seemed like forever before finally swooshing through the net.

"You still don't think we did it on our own?" Edge asked as Bond stepped in and grabbed the ball.

"No, we played well," said Lucas, smiling. "But my awesome underwear trick and that dot you showed me behind your ear at the party *might* have helped. I guess we'll never know!"

Bond took a shot that bounced off the pole, and then another that was off the backboard and in. "I'm just warming up," she said, sticking out her tongue like Beatrice, even though she knew none of her teammates would laugh at her.

Sports really are something, Edge thought to himself as he watched his friends take their shots. Hockey didn't just live in an arena or in the sound of a really great slapshot—he'd felt this for a long time. It lived in the hearts of every single player who played the game—however, wherever, and whenever they played.

"Hey, did you hear Connor at the party?" Lucas asked, suddenly laughing. "He yelled, 'Poopy baby bum!' at the top of the lungs whenever he got near the trophy. *So embarrassing.*"

"Yeah, Shayna and Nolan's cousins thought he was hilarious," said Swift, standing and grabbing Bond's rebound. The cousins had flown in from Eabametoong First Nation to do something on Parliament Hill—something about water—and they'd giggled at Connor's jokes all evening.

"Yeah, that was ridiculous—your brother's so funny!" said a voice from the schoolyard gates, suddenly joining in.

All the Chips turned.

It was Slapper.

This was supposed to be a secret meeting, thought Edge, who'd wanted to talk about Scratch's glitches with his teammates. *Now what are we going to do?*

Edge also had something else to tell them—well, to tell Lucas—but he'd been waiting for the right moment.

Bond rolled her eyes. She'd been waiting for a moment, too. Now she couldn't talk to the leaping Chips about how she'd known *where* Isobel's leap would happen. When they'd passed by the display case at the beginning of Isobel's tour, Bond could have sworn she'd seen Scratch's reflection in the glass. She'd convinced herself it was just a lighting trick, but when they'd looked at it the second time, she'd seen him again and known for sure—the wormhole was in the hallway of Rideau Hall.

"So who's signed up for HOCKEY CAMP?" Slapper asked, flicking one of his hockey cards against the gate. He was expecting to hear a half-dozen voices shout, "Me! Me! Me!"

"Of course I'm going—*duh*. I signed up the very first day!" said Lucas, excited, as he passed the ball to Edge. He liked basketball, but he *loved* hockey—and he looked forward to hockey camp almost as much as he looked forward to the Chips' regular season. There was nothing cooler than a hot summer morning in a skating rink, followed by an afternoon at a pool. *Nothing*.

He'd seen Shayna and Nolan at sign-up, and

Blades, Swift, Mouth Guard, and Dynamo had been talking about it for weeks. But this was the first time he'd realized that Edge hadn't mentioned it—not even on their late-night comm-call.

"You're going, too, right?" Lucas asked, turning to Edge, who'd just made another basket. *Edge loves hockey camp, too. Why hasn't it come up?*

"I'm, uh . . ." Edge started, but he wasn't sure how to say it. The sky was blue, the grass was getting greener, and in fact, since their call last night, he hadn't been thinking about hockey at all.

Lucas squinted. He could swear Edge's face looked just as it had back in that fishing shack on the canal.

"Well, *I'm* not going to hockey camp," Crunch suddenly blurted as he put his tablet in his bag and came to join the other kids on the court. "I'm going to science camp—well, crime scene investigation camp. While you're practising your slapshot, I'll be investigating murders."

"Real murders?" asked Bond, shocked.

"Fake ones," said Crunch, adjusting his glasses. "Mysteries. But I'll be taking fingerprints and analyzing the scene . . . I'll basically be a cop by the time we're back at school in September."

"And you, Edge?" Lucas asked, grabbing the ball and holding it as he looked at his best friend.

Edge took a breath, knocked the ball out of Lucas's hands, and got it in the hoop by throwing it backwards over his shoulder. "I'm . . ." he started, hanging his head and scrunching up his nose. "I'm going to *basketball camp* this summer."

"You're WHAT?!" Lucas said, shocked, but he didn't have time to say anything else.

BZZZZZZZZZZZZ!

Mouth Guard had buzzed him and was already shouting through his comm-band.

"Jared told on us! He told Coach Small and Quiet Dave about the cup!" Mouth Guard blurted. He was panicked and barely pausing between his words. "And your dad talked to Quiet Dave—about the machine he helped Crunch fix—"

"WHAT?!" Edge, Lucas, and Swift all shouted into Lucas's comm-band.

"Dave knows we've been leaping—he put it all together," said Mouth Guard.

"We're at the basketball court. Come over here— *fast!*" said Edge, looking at Slapper out of the corner of his eye and hoping the Chips' blabbermouth didn't say more over the comm-band.

"No, *you* get to the rink—*NOW!*" Mouth Guard said, his voice almost shaking. "I'm almost there. That's where they're waiting for us. We're in big, big trouble."

"What's *that* all about?" asked Slapper calmly, checking if his comm-band had also received a call.

But the others were already on their way to the arena.

ACKNOWLEDGEMENTS

Thanks to Suzanne Sutherland for her amazing, Dominion Cup–worthy editing skills; to Maeve O'Regan in publicity for her enthusiasm; and to Senior Editorial Director Jennifer Lambert for her support. And thanks to the rest of the team at HarperCollins, who helped us hoist our Stanley Cup and carry it along: Janice Weaver, our careful copyeditor; Stephanie Conklin, our extraordinary production editor; and Lloyd Davis, our wonderful proofreader. Thank you also to Bruce Westwood and Meg Wheeler at Westwood Creative Artists for their representation, guidance, and friendship.

Thanks to the many friends and new acquaintances who lent us their stories (and read some of ours) so we could shape the characters of the Singh family and Nolan and Shayna Atlookan: Manmeet Singh and his wife, Harprit Kaur, for sharing some Sikh family stories; the hosts of *Hockey Night in Canada:*

Punjabi Edition for their inventive calls; Sam Menard, Hallie Cotnam, Rumnik Chana (and her sons Hazoor and Nihal)—a few of our favourite hockey parents; Mandi Duhamel, the Canadian Regional Director, Youth Hockey, with the NHL; and Jeff Bignell, a former player on the Canadian Deaf Hockey Team. Miigwetch to Allison Norman, Leo Atlookan, and Kyle Jamieson, for their help with Shayna and Nolan.

Thank you also to Kim Smith, whose unbeatable illustrations should have a trophy case all their own.

And thank you to our families, who are the most precious prizes of all.

ROY MACGREGOR AND KERRY MACGREGOR

Many thanks to Roy MacGregor and Kerry MacGregor for creating an another magical story to illustrate; to Suzanne Sutherland, for her critical eye; and to Kelly Sonnack, my wonderful agent.

KIM SMITH

Roy MacGregor, who was the media inductee into the Hockey Hall of Fame in 2012, has been described by the *Washington Post* as "the closest thing there is to a poet laureate of Canadian hockey." He is the author of the internationally successful Screech Owls hockey mystery series for young readers, which has sold more than two million copies and is also published in French, Chinese, Swedish, Finnish, and Czech. It is the most successful hockey series in history—and is second only to *Anne of Green Gables* as a Canadian book series for young readers—and, for two seasons, was a live-action hit on YTV. MacGregor has twice won the ACTRA Award for best television screenwriting.

Kerry MacGregor is co-author of the latest work in the Screech Owls series. She has worked in news and current affairs at the CBC, and as a journalist with the *Toronto Star*, the *Ottawa Citizen*, and many other publications. Her columns on parenting, written with a unique, modern perspective on the issues and interests of today's parents, have appeared in such publications as *Parenting Times* magazine.

Kim Smith is an illustrator from Calgary. She is the *New York Times*-bestselling illustrator of over thirty picture books, including *Boxitects*, the Builder Brother series, and the Pop-Classics picture book adaptations of popular films, including *Back to the Future*, *Home Alone*, and *E.T. the Extra-Terrestrial*. Growing up, Kim's favourite hockey player was Lanny McDonald. She still admires his iconic moustache to this day.